The Man Who Heard the Land

NATIVE 🦅 VOICES

Native peoples telling their stories, writing their history

The Man Who Heard the Land

Diane Glancy

MINNESOTA HISTORICAL SOCIETY PRESS

Native Voices

Native peoples telling their stories,
writing their history

*To embody the principles set forth by the series,
all Native Voices books are emblazoned with a
bird glyph adapted from the Jeffers Petroglyphs
site in southern Minnesota. The rock art there
represents one of the first recorded voices of Native
Americans in the Upper Midwest. This symbol
stands as a reminder of the enduring presence of
Native Voices on the American landscape.*

Publication of Native Voices is supported in
part by a grant from The St. Paul Companies.

www.mnhs.org/mhspress

Manufactured in the United States of America

10 9 8 7 6 5 4 3 2 1

International Standard Book Number
0-87351-471-3 (cloth)

♾ The paper used in this publication meets
the minimum requirements of the American
National Standard for Information Sciences
—Permanence for Printed Library Materials,
ANSI Z39.48-1984.

*Library of Congress Cataloging-in-Publication
Data available on request.*

for Ursula Kohler
who asked for a green novel

for those who live without what was

I was as distant from myself as a hawk from the moon.
: James Welch, *Winter in the Blood*

God used to pay attention is what I'm saying.
: Louise Erdrich, *Love Medicine*

Remember O Lord, what is come upon us;
    consider, and behold our reproach.
Our inheritance is turned over to strangers,
    our hopes to aliens.
We are orphans and fatherless;
    our mothers are like widows.
We have drunk our water for money;
    our wood is sold unto us.
Our necks are under persecution;
    we labor, and have no rest.
    : *Lamentations 5:1–5*

The Man Who Heard the Land

Speak to the earth, and it shall teach you.

: Job 12:8

THE MAN WHO HEARD THE LAND WAS NOT FARMING, was not hunting, was not gathering wood for the log pile beside the house, but was an ordinary man driving on a highway, and the car stopped, and he heard the land. He thought it might have been the wind he heard, but he knew it was the land. He couldn't understand the words, but he knew the land was speaking.

Actually, the car didn't stop; he stopped it, because steam poured from beneath the dashboard, because hot water poured on his feet. Before the steam and the water poured out, the temp-gage light had gone on, had been on, but the mechanic said he was low on coolant, and filled the radiator reservoir. But when he saw steam under the dashboard, and felt the hot water on his ankles and in his shoes, he jerked his feet to cool them, and hit his knees against the steering wheel as he braked and pulled off the road and hopped from the car.

But what did the land say? The thunder and sky that were part of the earth, the wind currents pushed by the ocean, all of them together.

He walked to a station a half-mile ahead, his feet stinging in his shoes, and called a tow truck. The car had picked the right place to break down. He had turned north on Minnesota Highway 33 off 28, and was close to I-94. Osakis was just three miles beyond the interstate. He faced away from passing traffic when he returned to the car. At least it was summer, and not twenty below. He felt self-conscious as he waited, like he was a boy in front of his father's church in Osakis, his father and mother and the small congregation watching him sing. He wished he was in his old bed with the cowboy bedspread. The brown figures riding over him at night. The distant thunder mumbling.

Sometimes the earth sounded like someone talking in slow motion or at the wrong speed, or like someone who was deaf, or someone speaking in tongues. He could hear what it said, but not understand.

The silences were also a part of the voice. He saw the rows of trees by the highway. It was as if they walked on their toes to stand between the fields. "You line dancers," he said before he knew what he said.

He was on the way to meet his father; and now he would be late, or possibly even miss him. How strange time seemed. His father had asked him to a consultation about his mother. She couldn't care for the house any longer. He was making arrangements for her at the Manor. Should he join her? He didn't want to eat alone, sleep alone. He didn't want her to be alone.

The voice of the land moved over the road. It was a call when he needed someone coming. The voice of the land came from far away. It came from inside his head. It seemed a dream. The unconscious of the forest. The sub-conscious of the trees. What was the difference? Was the voice his own unconscious?

His father would have to decide about his mother by himself, he thought as he waited. How ineffectual he had been at times. He'd wanted to do something, but it didn't work. He showed up too late, or went the wrong way, or didn't see what he should have done until afterwards.

The trees were a seed inside a sail. He would say things like that because he heard the earth say it. Look at the samaras whirlygig in the air.

Where else would he have gotten such things? He, of few words. How often he stayed to himself. Maybe it was his comments that people didn't understand. Why did he say those things? Because they were on his mind to say. He had to say something. He couldn't just stand there while conversation was taking place and not say anything. Seeds falling to the earth did have trees inside them. But people didn't get what he meant. He knew they thought he was strange. He heard them once when they didn't know he could hear. He remembered his mother telling him to make himself clear. Why didn't he explain what he meant? Why didn't he speak more to the point?

Maybe the separation he felt was because he was adopted. He'd always known about it. He did not belong to his parents. He didn't know where he came from. An Indian mother, possibly, as best as they could guess. She left him. At the church. He thought of her in fragments because they fit the way he felt. Why had an Indian girl left her baby at a church?

The voice of the land was a way of knowing. But what did he know? He had heard the floods and tornadoes, the cruelty of the winters. He knew the cruelty of boys when he'd been a boy. He knew the cruelty of men. Sometimes he wished he didn't hear the land.

His feet throbbed as he waited for the truck to pull his car to the garage. He would call his father from there. Maybe he would leave a message, if he had missed him. There was some sort of fear forming inside his head. Not the wind or the possibility of being caught in the rain, or robbed while he waited for the tow truck.

His father had been a minister in Osakis, Minnesota. He had a small congregation, and farmed the field by the parsonage during the week, stopping sometimes in the middle of work to visit a family who'd lost a child, or had an accident, or a death, and it was up to his father to say something.

Then there were the long winters. The spring floods. His father had talked about the curse of the land. Had his father ever heard the land? No. His father and mother just heard the stillness of the house.

His parents lived meagerly. They had a poor congregation. Their lack of possessions was habitual. It was a dispensation from God. It was one of God's blessings.

But his fear wasn't about his parents either.

He remembered his closet had been an empty room, a place where he could go and listen to the stillness. If he covered the crack under his door with his shirts and trousers, he was in complete darkness.

His father had worked the fields, or read in his study all day, and at night, he heard his parents pray. They prayed for others more than themselves. The boy couldn't help them, but stayed in bed in his cold room, bending his toy man, Gumby, and the horse, Pokey.

Finally, the tow truck came. He stood awkwardly beside the highway as the car was hooked to the truck.

He was quiet as he rode to the garage in Osakis. Maybe the driver thought he was preoccupied. Maybe he was a man of few words himself.

His feet were still stinging from the hot water. But they felt more like they were cold. He remembered the winters he'd played outside too long, and when he came in the house, his feet throbbed just like they did now.

It was the heater coil that broke. It couldn't be fixed that day. The estimate was twelve hundred dollars.

The tow truck driver took him to a car rental. He left a message for his father at the Manor while he waited for a rental car.

Then he drove to his parents' house, where his father had returned. They talked at the dining room table as he removed his wet shoes and socks. For the first time, his mother was not there to set a plate in front of him.

His father asked about his job, his wife. He was an adjunct lecturer at the University of Minnesota in Morris. In reading, he had discovered environmental studies and various combinations of literature and naturalism, which he combined in a course called, "Literature and the Environment." For some reason, the students liked his detached imagination and the possibilities he opened for them, and his classes enrolled enough students that he continued teaching.

He also made trips to conferences no one else wanted to attend, or he was chosen by the department head to go, because no one was jealous of him. He had a small collection of foreign coins he showed his father.

He also traveled on his own when he could, maybe because he never went anywhere as a child. He would go to an antique store in Moorhead, Minnesota, or a bookstore in St. Paul. His wife worked. They didn't have children. She didn't seem to mind if he was gone for a while.

The weather was unsettled for June. It had been cold one week and hot the next, shifting suddenly and unexpectedly between them. There were grass fires. The earth seemed jerked one way, then the other. The land was skittish. The trees and lakes had choppy movements. There had been tornadoes. A farmer's barn would be gone. A shed roof would disappear.

Why was his mind wandering, jumping here and there? He realized he was uncomfortable with his father, without his mother between them, in the dining room. He had been raised by his parents, protected from hard decisions and realities they felt a child shouldn't know. He had been absorbed by his parents. He was now in his early thirties. Had he ever been anything but an extension of them?

As a boy, he had gone fishing in Lake Osakis. He'd gone hunting. But he stayed back from the boys when they tortured an animal. He remembered the angry protest of the animal, its fear, its pain, its whimpers, finally its death. He knew the trees held up the sky. Otherwise it would fall on him, crushing him, and the boys who had been cruel, wherever they were now.

Where was the bicycle he rode on Nokomis Street into Osakis? The Saturday matinees at the Empress Theater on Central, which had closed? Was it waiting for him? That's what heaven was. The return to a self-absorbed life.

His father talked about the land as a struggle. He had called him back to work if he watched a blackbird with a yellow beak on the fence.

It was hard for him to sit at the table. He was supposed to respond to his father's concerns, but he couldn't. He wanted to get up from the table and go to his own house, where maybe his wife would have supper.

His wife was an accountant. She worked with numbers. Her feelings were her own. They were not like the couple they had heard arguing in the next apartment, then loving later. Finally, they had been able to afford a small house of their own.

He remembered staying home while his father went to see the people in his congregation, or if he went with his father when he made a call, he had stayed in the car. Had he played the radio? No. His father only had a radio in the car to listen to the weather. What had he done? How could he have spent all that time waiting and not remember anything in particular? Not even sleeping. But in some subconscious state, he heard the hissing of the trees.

How often had he made a decision, then done something else? If he had decided to tell his father what the boys were doing, he didn't tell. If he decided he would tell the boys to leave the animal alone, he wouldn't. Later, it was the same. If he wanted to tell his wife something, he wouldn't. If he wanted to bring up a difficult issue in his class, he didn't. He tossed like a bird on the air currents.

He thought of the church where his father preached. It was a small building on Second Street off Main, with a plain wall behind the pulpit. How many years had he stared at the scars and uneven places exposed by the sun while his father preached? What had his father preached? Salvation through Christ. It was words to him.

His father sat at the table with his head in his hands. His wife had to stay at the Lutheran Manor. That was no longer the question. But he'd decided to move to the Manor with her. That was the decision he wanted to talk about.

"What will you do with the house?" he asked his father.

"It belongs to the church. The new minister lives in the new parsonage. We've been allowed to stay in the old parsonage as long as we wanted."

The compensation for being a minister all those years was residency at the retirement manor the church owned, or rather the denomination owned.

The care of his parents without cost, or minimal cost, was a sizable consideration.

Yes, he seemed to remember now. There would be no messy sales. The house would be left to the church. Just a few pieces of furniture to get rid of; maybe he could just leave them in the house for the church. Then there were personal articles and clothing they would take to the Manor with them. He listened to his father talk of the years in the house. He knew he'd have to sit and listen until his socks dried, or he could borrow a pair of his father's. He looked at his watch.

He remembered his mother in the kitchen. His father in the small room he called his study. It was just a bedroom that could have been used for a sister, or other children, or a guest room. But there were no other children. When someone stayed with them, he had given up his bed and slept on a cot in the kitchen. He remembered the dull, slow, silent life of the house. But outside, he heard the voice of the land. He tried to remember what it said.

The house seemed narrow. It was as if the walls had pressed the sides of his bed with its cowboy spread into a small corral where his Gumby toy had kept Pokey, his horse. He remembered how he'd lived in his imagination, in being someplace other than where he was. He remembered how he'd bent Gumby into different shapes, Gumby not protesting.

Yes, he had waited in the car while his father was talking to someone in grief. His mother was at home fixing their supper, which they would eat in silence, unless his father wanted to talk about the sorrow he brought into the house.

He lived in an interior place. What was he thinking? his parents sometimes asked. But they seemed satisfied that everything was as it should be. He would not give them trouble like other children gave their parents. He was a testimony to them.

Why did they need the church? Couldn't his father just have farmed? Surely there was no income from the church. Whatever came in went out again to others, to the widow whose children didn't have shoes to wear to school, or coats when the weather turned cold. The teachers told them who didn't have lunch. His mother sent food with him for others. Sometimes she came with a pan of cookies.

He was embarrassed over the conversation with his father. What did his father want? What was he supposed to do? He'd always been treated as a child. Now he was supposed to discuss a matter with his father as an equal? Was that the vague fear inside his head? He would have to be responsible? Was it himself he feared? But his parents loved him. He was their only child.

But what was love? Who was Christ? This man who sat in heaven and looked down on them? He remembered sitting on the edge of the pond, watching the fish and the movement he had set in motion with a crumb thrown in the water. He thought of a hook in the mouth of the fish, or the hook swallowed and caught inside.

He thought sometimes his father loved the incomprehensible world. He seemed to wait for trouble. He worked to invent ways to explain God in the mystery and misery they knew in their small town.

Far away his wife was growing up. Maybe she and her father sat together reading of an evening. The sisters upstairs listening to the radio, calling their boyfriends, her mother reading movie magazines, while his wife did her math homework, seeing how the numbers worked, how they were as pliable as Gumby in her hands, how she could sink into them as if they were dishwater.

He stood back and watched others. The boys in trouble. His parents in their silent marriage. His father in the pulpit. His mother hanging clothes on the line. The women talking in the yard. The men in the store. Day after day. Who were they? How could they move through his life without his feeling anything for them? He'd heard his father pray. His mother also. Sometimes someone would come by the house. They would talk in hushed voices from his father's study, sharing some secret that had to be told as quietly as possible. Otherwise it would spill into the imagination of the others, where it would take root and replicate itself.

He could feel the drafty house. Sometimes he sat with his cap on. How the wind seemed to move through the house. It had its own secret passage.

But how could the land have words? Maybe he just imagined the voice. What did it say, anyway?

All he heard when he listened was the stillness, the holy stillness, full of shelves of angels God took down when he needed them, wound them with the key in their back like his father wound the clock every Saturday night, tightly, and the wings would whirl, and toss the angels down to earth where they were needed. Mr. Standt's field, where a brushfire threatened his barn and small herd of livestock, Mrs. Albert's heart, which pumped in her chest with a swallowing sound he could hear in church, Fred Robley's wife, whom his father spoke about in a hushed voice.

He remembered his father talking about the Bible. It seems as though Noah, Jonah, and David walked through the parsonage. But the bosom of Abraham. What was that? The lungs? Chest? The abstraction of an idea? A room, a study in God's house not used for anything else, with a name, Abraham's bosom, on it, like the church where his father preached, but didn't get paid? Was it someplace where the dead waited in some dull room for an unknown afterlife possibly equally drab?

Was Abraham's bosom like his drafty room?

At least it wasn't hot. Those who ignored the mighty God would roast, his mother had said, and nothing they could do after this life could change it. He thought of the hot car-radiator water pouring on his feet. How red his feet were when he finally took off his shoes and socks in his father's house. He could still feel the sting on his ankles and feet. How would he like that over his whole body? he could almost hear his mother ask.

He could see the trails of smoke rising from those people in hell, like smoke from the chimneys in Osakis in winter.

As soon as God replicated himself in him, by his acceptance of Christ as his Savior, and he replicated himself in his children, he had completed his earthly task.

He thought sometimes his parents longed for death. It seemed what they waited for in the house after supper.

His mother had said she wanted grandchildren, but when they didn't come, she reminded herself of all the messes they would make. But he didn't want children. Neither did his wife. What was the point? There were enough children, too many children. They were noisy and troublesome; they were draining. He had heard his parents' concern over him. How they saved for his education. How they watched what they said in front of him. He was something they had to step around to be themselves.

One summer his wife's niece had stayed with them, sleeping in his wife's workroom. His wife had been apprehensive, nervous, but he encouraged her. It was a strain and they were both relieved when the girl left, but he had liked hearing the piano. His mother felt a house had to have a piano, and insisted they have one, but the girl was the only one who played it.

He had taken piano lessons, but his teacher had moved. He remembered walking across the yard with the wind picking up the leaves, knowing he'd never have to play again.

He had attended his wife's niece's recital in Moorhead. There had been a vase of flowers on the black piano. A white wall behind her as she played. In her music, he had heard the land; dust on a road, the sun sinking behind the earth, the moon in the dark sky, a field of water after rain.

But what had he recognized? Listening to her music, he had felt a stirring of feeling. He had wanted to put the feeling away. It was as if the land gave him an awareness. It was an augmentation or development of some part of himself. But the land was here to be dominated, his father had preached. Why should he listen to its voice? Because it knew things he didn't.

He remembered the few times he'd seen his father stirred. Once his father had hit the pulpit with his fist over some point he was trying to make. He didn't want to be bothered about anyone or anything. He just wanted to live without trouble, without meaning, without God and Jesus and the Holy Ghost, and angels and cherubim, and seraphim and saints, without the whole chain of his father's beings. He only wanted to be away from them all. He had wanted to dry the dishes, put the pans away, and go to his room. He would read, or play with his lead soldiers and horses, or Gumby and Pokey, or roll his marbles, or be filled with the duty of being.

Somehow his boyhood passed. He went to Concordia College in Moorhead and met his wife and married her. They shared their lives without passion. They were comforted by it, except in the night when he roamed in a landscape inside himself, and heard the clumps of trees on the horizon, the stumps in the fields, saying in his dreams, *I give you the air you breathe.* And his wife would nudge him and tell him to turn over.

Now he sat with his father at the table as his voice trailed off over the painting of Sennacherib. Awkwardly, he put his hand on his father's shoulder while his father sobbed.

He was glad to be gone from his father's house. He read the trees as he drove barefooted back to Morris in the rental car. The trees passed like pages in a book. Speed-reading, he didn't get it all, but he knew they had a story.

He was satisfied with the flicker of his wife's existence when she cooked and washed for him, and together they paid for their small, three-bedroom house and his car, then hers. Their needs were few, and they had a savings account. He had nothing bothering him. He liked the quiet passing of his days. He taught summer school. He mowed the lawn, or tried to get the grass to grow under the fir tree in the yard, or thought he would paint the trim on the house. He was on a journey, as his father had preached, but he didn't know where he was going. He often felt as if he was someone other than who he was.

His wife's sisters seldom came for a visit when he was there. They were noisy and boisterous, and had troubled families. Just look at how they handled their lives. He and his wife viewed them from a distance, his wife holding on to him the few times they felt the need to be close. Then she gardened while he cleaned out the garage or basement, or graded papers or read a book on the environment in his study, while she worked in hers. He was as tidy as she was, and their lives were their own.

He was uncomfortable around his wife's sisters. He liked the niece who had stayed with them, the one who played the piano. His wife must be like her father. He died soon after they met, and he hadn't had time to know him, but from what he heard from the mother and daughters, he must have been a man something like himself. Maybe that's why his wife married him. She was more like the father, and her sisters were more like the mother.

He wondered what they said behind his back. Once he heard them laughing after he left the room.

How can a man justify God in his pitiful condition on earth? He would take God out of the sky and put him in the house next door where they fought all day. Let him be a helpless child in that house, or the dog in the backyard they often forgot to feed or water.

The earth spoke to him in his dreams. The voice of the land moved like a dream. It seemed to say, there were distortions in his perceptions. But what did that mean? He woke in the night. The hands of the earth were pushing him down. Its voice was a dream he couldn't follow. His eyes were small round balls on his face. His eyebrows, small worms. His legs were as wide as his father's field. His feet as large as tractors he could hear in someone else's fields.

He felt pulled away from his father and mother. His feelings seemed to unfold like newspapers.

He drove to Osakis and returned the rental car, but the garage had found something else wrong with his car, and he had to come back the next day.

He called his wife. She would meet him at the Manor, where he would walk to visit his mother. He knew his father would be there also.

After their visit, he watched his wife take the steering wheel with a tight grip as they started back to Morris. What if the land was like the wheel, steering him somewhere? The steering wheel was round, but it didn't roll like the tires. But it turned the car.

Now he was late for a department meeting, but it didn't matter. They weren't supposed to have meetings in the summer anyway. But there were a few matters to be worked out. A position they thought they had filled was suddenly vacant. He had to teach a composition course he didn't want. There was the rearrangement of another professor's classes. He always sat at the end of the table, just inside the door.

He was not inarticulate, or invisible, or nameless, but inaudible. He felt sometimes he held his own heart in his hand. He felt sometimes, it, alone, was his companion.

He arrived at the parsonage early on Saturday morning. His father was ready to move, his face red, his grief showing, though he'd probably been in prayer since dawn. He laid his father's suit and a few shirts on hangers in the backseat. He carried a box of books to the trunk of his car. Another box of underwear, pajamas, a small leather kit of personal articles. He guessed his father didn't even have a suitcase as he helped him down the steps and into the front seat. Only once did he hear a stifled sob.

After moving his father into the Manor with his mother, he cleaned out the attic, the garage, the basement, of lifetime possessions, most of which were his, other than boxes of his mother's recipes and kitchen things. A few trunks of his father's books. His own sled and ice skates. A small wooden box of fishing lures. A box of newspaper articles of religious interest. Record snows. There was the painting of King Sennacherib, which he'd remembered since he was a boy. Old clothing and shoes that he donated to the poor, but maybe even the poor didn't want them.

He left his parents' seventeen-year-old car in the garage. It belonged to the church also.

He brought one of his father's trunks to his attic. And the painting of Sennacherib. The trunk held letters and old sermons, besides a few books. There wasn't room for it at the Manor and his father wanted to keep it. One of the books in the trunk was his, *More Things Any Boy Can*

Make, by Joseph Leeming. He read it one evening until his wife called him down from the attic.

It was fifty miles from Morris to Osakis. His wife agreed to go with him to see his parents on Saturday mornings. She even cut some roses to take to them.

His mother was as pliable as Gumby. She was waiting in her walker, which he wanted to call Pokey. She was hateful to him. His gentle mother. Had he ever heard her raise her voice? Where did he get that feeling? What had she ever shown him but kindness? What had she ever said but warnings so he could escape or bypass troubles?

They sat in his parents' room. What would they say? What language would come? He waited for his father to speak. He talked about getting settled. His mother's face was docile. Was she still in her head? Yes. She looked at his father as if she were still serving him, as if they were in their small kitchen with the study in the other room, just on the other side of the kitchen. Her dishes in the cupboard, her apron over the chair.

His wife sat in the chair as if she listened. She would dutifully go anywhere with him. She kept the world numbered for him. He could move from one place to the next because it followed logically and in numerical order.

But sometimes he felt the order disordering. He didn't know where he came from. His birth was in a compartment separate from his life. He didn't have to think about it. Feel. He had been abandoned. Left behind. He was probably Indian. He had dark hair and eyes. There was something that made his parents think he was. There was a girl they remembered. Dakota, probably. She'd been pregnant. Then they found a baby at the church. And they never saw her again. But he was probably more of a mixed heritage. It made him shudder. He pulled away from his thoughts. Why did he let that memory into his head? Why did he remember those pieces? Because they were all he had. They made stepping stones away from the unknown.

He watched the trees from the window, but he didn't want to hear the land. Was the land an orphan too? Was it something other than it had to be? He worked to push his thoughts aside. They made him feel something other than himself. Something of which he was not a part, a separation that he'd always felt.

A few people shuffled by the room at the Manor and his father commented on them. He felt his feet twitch as if they remembered the hot water from the car.

He saw there were thorns on the roses like Gumby's triangular nose. He remembered his mother cutting the noses off. Why had she clipped the thorns before placing the roses from her trellis in a vase? She had castrated the noses from the roses. She had castrated anything, he thought, that didn't fit her idea of gentleness.

He remembered a tree split by lightning.

He lived on the topsoil. How shallow he'd been. His understanding was limited. Things were outside him. They were other than he was. They went on without him. He hadn't realized. If he listened to the earth, he would know what he'd tried not to know. He was a responsible being with ears that heard the earth on which he walked. And further, the man who heard the land would hear himself.

As he sat in his parents' room at the Manor, he remembered his parents' house; the yard, the flowery bed that had looked like eraser streaks on the blackboard when he squinted.

He had closed one eye and walked.

Sometimes, he thought, the sky had been on a bicycle. Had been a bicycle. He saw the few hairs on his arms like trees under his magnifying glass.

He had a whirling whistle, a jumping peanut, handcuffs, Scripture cards. He remembered he'd made the cards stand up; he'd clothespinned them to his bike wheels until his father saw how he used Scriptures and punished him, the only time he'd been seriously punished.

He remembered the plain walls of his parents' house, the rug with fringe that spilled on the floor. It reminded him of the early photo of the church in his father's office; the raw land without bushes, shrubs, any sort of landscape.

There was also the painting of Sennacherib, king of Assyria, on the wall. He thought about history. Sennacherib had conquered the land from the Mediterranean to Egypt. Why had his parents had Sennacherib on their wall?

It sounded like a cough syrup to him. It looked like *cherub*, an angel's friend. But it was pronounced *kur-rib*. He thought of the difference between a steering wheel and the four wheels that were the tires of a car.

He squinted to read the handwriting, *I will cut down the tall cedars and the firs. I have dried up the rivers of besieged places.* Isaiah 37:24-25. He had heard his father preach about Sennacherib. No enemy could defeat the Lord and his people, not even a destroyer like Sennacherib.

Once when his parents were outside, the boys had been in his house, looking at the picture, talking about ravished women.

But when Sennacherib's army was camped to war against Hezekiah, king of Judah, seven hundred years before Christ, the Lord God had killed thousands of Sennacherib's men. The Bible said, *He smote the camp of the Assyrians.* But then, when Sennacherib returned to Ninevah, his own sons murdered him. Or when it became confused in his mind, *their son murdered them*, he thought it said.

He was lost in thought when he felt his wife pull his arm. It was time to go. Lunch was going to be served in the Manor. They would see his parents again next Saturday.

And the Lord said . . . I must go down and see whether they have done altogether according to the outcry which has come unto me. Genesis 18:21–22

That was God speaking. The Almighty, High-in-the-Heavens Lord, who made the sky and earth, the whole universe, and he had to make a trip to earth to find out what he wants to know? He-Who-Knows-All-Things had a weedy beginning, it seemed to him. Then later, in the nineteenth chapter of Genesis, two angels showed up in Sodom and stayed with Lot. And what the Lord heard was true. But what was meaningful to him is that God traveled in the personage of two angels to see if what he heard was true. He traveled in otherness, in other words. The way the sound of *cherub* changed according to what context it was in.

He thought the land spoke like that. Shifting as it was shifted. The earth spoke with many voices, many speeches, not always agreeing, but there was a multiplicity in the landscape. Something changing and not absolute.

The summer moved into August, and then late August. He sat in his office in the English department at the University of Minnesota at Morris preparing for classes. He read a new anthology on nature writing for his "Literature and the Environment" course. He thought about ideas.

In September, when the fall quarter began, he had to face his new classes. He wanted to feel like his father before his congregation. But he didn't have the confidence. Entering his classes for the first time was like jumping into Lake Osakis as a boy, not knowing where he'd come up, or if he would, his heart beating outside his chest. But he closed the door behind him and surfaced with his usual shortness of breath as he began to talk. Soon his breathing returned to normal, though he would fumble somewhat all quarter.

The two lecturers with whom he shared an office began keeping regular hours, and soon he sat in the crowded office reading papers from his composition and literature courses. He tried to keep his mind on his grading. He wanted to guide the new academic year in the right direction. But the voices in the papers pushed him toward an intersection in his own thoughts, where the voices of the students and the voices of the land communicated their concerns for survival. But there had to be more than survival.

He realized it was nearly time for another department meeting he would have to attend, and his colleagues would talk about things he didn't know were going on, but would have to find out, and act interested in, all under the notice of his department head.

At night, he continued reading the book he found stored with his father's papers and sermons. *More Things*

Any Boy Can Make, by Joseph Leeming. He had brought it down from the attic to his study.

He remembered the clothespin wrestlers and airplanes. He remembered *Multum in Parvo,* a multitude in a small place, which was a peep box, a shoe box, in which his lead soldiers were crowded together. He had poked a hole for light in one end of the box. He bought two mirrors at the Five and Dime and scraped the silvering from the back of one mirror. He glued the first over the hole at one end of the shoe box. He glued the other at the other end. He had made a hole in the lid for light. The soldiers multiplied when he looked in the box. He imagined wars.

Somehow they were talking about his mother. They were looking to him for his opinion. She was worse; should she be hospitalized? He didn't know where they were in their conversation.

Sometimes he stopped trying, and withdrew farther into himself.

"*In quietness and confidence will be your strength,* Isaiah 30:15," his mother had said. He had quietness, but not the confidence.

He remembered the line of trees in a field. "Toe dancers," he had called them.

Then he'd made a ring toss. He had wanted to make a coconut bird shelter, but his mother never bought a coconut.

On the way back to Morris from the Manor on another Saturday, he remembered the bucking bronco, the magic cars, the steam turbine made by boiling water in a baking-powder tin, with two pieces of tin notched together on a string, a hole in the lid, the steam turning the wheel. Had his mother let him use her stove? He couldn't remember. There was another project, something called, "Perpetual Motion," but his mother wouldn't let him burn a candle in his room. Maybe the land spoke in pockets of ideas and concentration like these games.

Later that night, he sat reading *More Things Any Boy Can Make*. Wishbone skipjacks. Mysterious mothball, which rose with soda-water gas bubbles to the surface, the gas escaping, the mothball sinking again.

He remembered he had wanted to read "How Magicians Make Handkerchiefs Disappear," but his mother saw the chapter and wouldn't let him. The *pull* up his sleeve was dishonest. Ungodlike, she said.

Now he and his father had to decide what to do with her again. Let them cover her with a handkerchief and let her disappear.

He spent the day writing a paper to give at a conference in Germany when the fall quarter was under way. It was about the depletion of natural resources, a corollary of literary theory and the loss of meaning for language. But language made its own world. It could be reconstituted with a *green perspective* before it was too late, before the environment was bankrupt.

He stayed in his study except to fix lunch, which he brought back to his study to eat by himself. His legs felt weak. He didn't feel good, he thought, though he was doing what he wanted to do. That evening, he and his wife had a light supper at Ardelle's on Atlantic Avenue near his small university. He had to pick up a book he forgot in his office anyway.

Later, she watched television in their bedroom while he sat in the living room for a while in thought.

He closed his eyes as the plane roared down the runway. *Reel us in,* he said to God as the plane was pulled into the sky on the end of a line, then let go.

He was on his way to Germany for a short conference. He knew it wasn't long enough to accomplish anything, but if his university was willing to pay, because they wanted him to develop an environmental studies course, then he would go.

His wife had driven him to the airport in Minneapolis, over 150 miles from Morris, with her sister and another niece who talked about shopping. After they let him out, he boarded the seven-hour, all-night flight to Amsterdam, then on to Berlin. His host was waiting. He had a Citroen with a gearshift in the dash. They traveled a narrow, winding road through a group of trees waving as if directing Wagner.

After a few hours' sleep, he took a long walk because he didn't want to talk to anyone at the conference yet. The trees spoke German and he couldn't understand. But one, he was sure, said, *the just shall live by faith*. Martin Luther had been the German author his father read.

His feet burned when he returned to his room. He remembered how he had scalded his feet, made them sensitive. He had limped into class for a week afterwards to lecture.

He stayed in an old hotel. The wood floor creaked. The light came under the door. The tall ceiling was halfway to the sky.

By then, his colleagues from other universities had arrived at the hotel. They took the lift to his floor, talking loudly at first, not knowing their voices went under the doors like water. Later they'd be quiet, so those spies behind doors wouldn't hear what they said.

The conference in Germany was on the environment. He watched the lecturers and assistant professors in the meeting rooms. They were overweight, underpaid. They were struggling for tenure, for publication, for recognition, feeling that their future was riding on the presentation of their conference papers.

If he could become permanent faculty, if he could get tenure, he could stop worrying about detail. He could research the voices of the forest.

He noticed the conference women at other tables. He left them alone. They seemed in a group of their own.

He imagined a man worked hard all day. At night his wife should support him with her food and love so he could go back to work another day. He felt women should help men, not threaten them and their possessions or positions.

In the morning, he heard the people cleaning their bowls with their spoons in the silent breakfast room. In one corner, there were a few professors talking about some matter. They were loud and gesturing with their spoons. But where he sat, it was like eating at his parents' house.

On another walk, in an antique shop he saw a metal deer that was a candleholder. "Fourteenth century," the shop owner said when he knew he was American. "Only a few left in museums. Twenty-four thousand deutsche marks."

If he could do anything, he'd travel, just travel. He wouldn't write articles, or lecture, or take photographs. He would be an observer, a hearer, a viewer of what happened. Not involved in what was happening. Traveling simply for the sake of it. *The inhabitable base of the earth is shrinking.* He's sure that's what the tree said as he passed.

Some were falling into the darkness over the edge of the earth. For a moment, he felt like he floated in that darkness. Maybe it was one of his father's old sermons he heard. They seemed to speak to him also.

The fish and birds were created on the fifth day, before the crowded sixth day of animals and man. Yes, he was hearing a fragment of one of his father's sermons.

He loved the word *Euphrates* in the Bible, because of the freight of it, the involvement of the sound, *you*, and the tension of the *tees*, which sounded like *trees*. The Euphrates was a river flowing west from the Persian Gulf through Iraq, Syria, and Turkey. It sounded far away. He remembered reading the large globe he had in his old room. He wished he was fishing in the Euphrates that afternoon.

You freight trees, he thought as he carried the thought of the trees; the weight and the message of them. They seemed to fill an emptiness in him; they seemed to walk with him.

He liked his paper. He liked giving it. He was nervous, but everyone was, reading what they had conjectured in their quiet studies in front of the audience and other presenters at the conference.

After the panel members gave their papers, the moderator asked for questions from the audience. The audience members leaned forward as they spoke, impressed with the importance of their own questions and the immediacy of their need for an answer. There was some banter; there was a puff of excitement, there was a gust of laughter as they reached an obvious, agreed-upon point. There was more nervousness from talking in front of peers. Maybe someone would correct them publicly, or uncover a flaw in their thinking. Others wanted to

speak, but the session was over and groups rushed together to talk or argue their point, while the next panel
and the next audience moved into the room, and the previous panel and audience had to move on to other panels or hallways or even cafés to talk further about their
suppositions and the theses they maintained.

But he withdrew from the groups, not that he was a
part of them anyway, and walked along a busy street
near the university in Berlin, thinking of the next paper
he would write. That's why he liked conferences. There
was fuel for further work.

Berlin was a city reunited with itself. But it was uncomfortable with its reuniting. He rode the trolley to east
Berlin. He saw the poverty, the dirtiness. Berlin was still
a place of opposites. The east looked back to socialism
when everyone owned everything and everyone was assured of work. People in the west now felt like they were
responsible for poor relatives.

For some reason, he remembered his niece's recital.
He had heard the land when she played. Maybe if he
heard music, he could understand the land in Germany.
But he saw the people throw trash on the ground. Maybe
the land was not speaking clearly because of their disre-
gard for it. Yet he heard a lecturer with a heavy accent re-
fer to a lake as the eye of their mother.

Even the trees coughed in the industrial pollution.
They turned brown beside the highways. He saw them
again on the way to the airport. It was the same in
America.

I used to be here, before houses and buildings and roads, this was mine, mine, this. It was the voice of the land he heard in his imagination. It was the land speaking. He knew it. He could give nothing to the land, except maybe his body, and even that would be put in a coffin and kept from the earth.

At the corner, a man next to him looked at him. Maybe he'd been talking to himself. Maybe the man recognized him as someone not from his country. Maybe the man would ask him for something. He moved across the street quickly when the light changed.

He could feel the land whisper to him. It wanted him to notice the way it looked under large cloud-bulks that moved across the city, slowly dropping shadow and light.

A soldier with a girl passed him on the street. For a moment he felt lonely for a woman. He missed his wife. He thought of her order. But no, he didn't want anything to do with love. Think how much room his wife's clothes took.

It was night in Minnesota where she was; she was sleeping, mumbling words to herself now and then. Time walked around the earth with its presence. There was an incomprehensibility that needed recognition, that made him feel disconnected and uncomfortable.

He thought of it after the conference in Berlin. He thought about it until he slept on the plane back to America, to Minnesota, to Minneapolis, then to Morris, then to the bed in his house like a single ripple on the sea.

Far below, the ocean spread beneath the plane. It was like he was in Abraham's bosom. It was as if the plane were an ice-fishing house and he stood over the ice hole. In his dreams, he entered the water as if he were a hook on the end of a line. The ocean nibbled his subconscious as he slept. He felt the light chop of the plane. The flight across time zones warped his perceptions. Mixed his boundaries. There was a voice saying, *What if time is not what you think?* He dreamed of millions of years pressed into a thousand. What if the inhabitable base of time was shrinking? Could time be an invention? Not as it seemed? What if the ages were only a few years? What if they only looked as far away as they were looked back to? What if there was a relativity that was not understood?

He woke from time to time and fell back into sleep among dreams of the ocean. He felt the fish were entering his mouth. He coughed, thinking there was a fish wiggling in his nose, but it was only the dry air in the plane.

When he returned to his house in Morris, his lawn was full of leaves. He raked them before he faced his classes, and before he went to the Manor with his wife to visit his parents. He could feel the days changing.

His dreams of the ocean slept while he was awake. But once in a while, he felt the piles of leaves he raked were fish. They also had blown under the fir tree beside his house. He got down and raked them out.

His father and mother were quiet when he and his wife visited the Manor. His wife was trying to knit a sweater. It gave her something to do. He watched her mouth move as she counted stitches.

When he had dated his wife at Concordia College in Moorhead, they'd gone to the Newman Society films. On her birthday, she took him to her parents' house near Moorhead. Her parents seemed to like him, or at least accept him. When she had complained of chills and went to her room, he continued to visit with her parents before he returned to his dormitory on the Concordia campus. He thought he'd wait a week to call her, and it wasn't until he saw her in the library with a cardigan over her shoulders held by a clasp and chain that he remembered he hadn't called.

Was it the same cardigan she wore as they talked with his parents? He looked at his wife as she frowned at the rows of her knitting.

When her father had died, she called, and he'd taken her to her mother's. The funeral had cemented their relationship.

He told his father about the metal deer candleholder he had seen in Germany. It cost more than his father had made in a year, but he didn't say that. His mother lay voiceless in bed. Once in a while her mouth moved as if she were talking to someone on the ceiling.

Why did he leave his wife behind when he traveled? his father asked.

"She has to work," he told his father. "You know that."

"It's all I can do to clean the house on Saturdays and leave Sunday to prepare for the week."

His father looked at her. "Sundays belong to the Lord," he said.

"We don't," she didn't finish.

"You don't go to church?" His father looked at them.

Sometimes he did, he assured his father.

"But sometimes he has papers to grade," his wife told her father-in-law. "Sometimes he works through the weekends."

"What time do you give God?"

He remembered as a child he pictured God as an attendance taker.

An old man wandered into his parents' room, looked at them, and walked out without saying anything.

After a while, it was time for them to leave.

They stopped at Don's Restaurant on Fifth Street when they returned to Morris, because it was open Saturday nights, but not through the week. He wife didn't enjoy cooking and it was convenient for them to meet after work and share their day as they ate. Usually they met at Ardelle's Eatery on Atlantic Avenue, or the Atlantic Avenue Family Restaurant. Sometimes, even, they ate at the Diamond Supper Club, or the Ranch House Restaurant, but not often. He didn't feel as comfortable at the nicer places. At Don's Restaurant, he ordered the walleye, wild rice, carrots, and sometimes the fries.

At the next table, he noticed the parents were concerned over their child. He watched them. Did they irritate him because it reminded him of his parents' concern over him? Or did he want his parents back to take care of him?

There was an environmental conference in Prague. It came during his fall break from classes. He wanted to attend. He had sent a paper last spring and it was accepted.

The university only paid for one trip, the department head told him, which he had already taken. But he would see what he could do about the university paying half, since the conference was on environmental studies. His department head also reminded him he was only adjunct faculty.

He had saved some money, worrying about his parents' retirement. Was the trip worth spending some of it? Now that his parents were in the Manor, and he had to a large extent been spared financial responsibility, he could use some of the money to travel.

He talked to his wife about it as they ate at Ardelle's.

Could they afford it?

If they didn't eat out so often, his wife said.

But they didn't like to cook. Didn't have time to cook. What else did they do?

"What does the trip involve?" his wife asked, nodding to someone across the room, maybe someone she knew through her work.

He would give a talk on a panel, but also had been asked to present a lecture in a class.

He told his wife they could visit Finland after the conference. It was where her great-great-grandparents were born. After some reluctance and worry, she agreed. For several weeks, he heard about her passport, her shopping for a proper suitcase, the articles of clothing and toiletries she would need, a new camera, a book to read.

She continued to worry about what she had brought as they traveled across the Atlantic to Amsterdam and across Europe to Prague.

Once they were in their hotel, she decided after he unpacked that they could get a better price in another room and he had to pack again and move to another floor.

She stayed behind his first day at the conference. She couldn't get used to the daylight when it was supposed to be night, she said.

At the university before his talk, he had to use the toilet. A professor with a key and a roll of toilet paper in his hand led him to the end of the hall past groups of students. Did he need to stand up or sit down? Just stand. He could do without the protocol; he just wanted to pass down the hall unnoticed, and not be led ceremoniously to the small toilets, the key jiggling in the professor's hand.

Before he lectured to the class, he took a drink of water, which he discovered was *with gas* as they called it, which made his throat itch, and he had to swallow and swallow as he talked. In the restaurant, he was given the same carbonated water when he just wanted water, good, cold tap water with an ice cube in it, and decaffeinated coffee, none of which they had, though they were trying to make him comfortable; they only made him more miserable. He was unhappy and supposed to be grateful for it.

The next day, a man next to him on the panel took longer than he was supposed to, inching into his time, stealing it. Was he like the land? Didn't the land have to sit there while others took what belonged to it? Didn't the land have to sit silently while everyone covered it with houses and buildings and pavement?

He grew nervous with anger. His wife was in her chair near the back. Was she concerned about his nervousness, or did she just sit there thinking of her numbers? Probably she was knitting; counting rows.

He had flood waters frozen within himself. If they thawed, he could be covered. Finally the man next to him finished, and after polite applause, he gave his paper until the time ran out.

The next morning, he started out with his wife and her guidebook. "With a thousand years of architecture untouched by natural calamity or war, Prague is a city where the entire history of Western civilization can be traversed, on foot, within the space of a few blocks. The Romanesque, Gothic, Baroque, Art Nouveau, Art Deco, and even the occasional Cubist structure coexist in a visual medley of historical styles."

They spent the day walking Prague. The river, the Charles Bridge.

He bought his wife a scarf, and a knit hat with a piano-key pattern for her niece. He looked at an iron ring from a horse's harness, but didn't buy it.

As he carried the sack with the niece's hat, he remembered the land he had heard in her music. Maybe the voice of the land was only a figment of his imagination.

He and his wife were always awkward, she going, he stopping, bumping against one another, full of indecision, confusion, as to what they wanted to do. Everyone else seemed to walk with a purpose. Everyone with a phone at their ear. How did they know that many people to talk to?

He looked at the nondescript buildings, the street cafés, gardens, fruit markets. More traffic. He heard music from a sidewalk mandolin. His wife was in her ugly walking shoes and jacket, her shoulder bag held tightly to her chest.

He crossed a cobblestone street, looked at signs he couldn't read, the strange combination of vowels and consonants.

Why had he brought his wife? Because he'd been

lonely on his last trip. Because a sailor had passed with his girl on a street in Berlin, and they'd made him think he wanted companionship. Because his father had asked, Why he didn't bring her?

He thought again of how much room his wife's clothes took, her underwear, her shoes. Her navies were different navies. None of them went together.

She took forever to decide to cross the street. He tripped on a broken curb. He couldn't understand what she said.

They spent time changing hotels, and rooms within those hotels, because she didn't like them, or thought they could get a better price.

They'd come to the conference in Prague a few days early to see antique shops and stores where she looked for souvenirs for her sisters, her nephews and nieces. But she was a walking accountant thinking of exchange rates, how much each step cost them. She talked of the dinginess of the buildings let go under the communist regime. She didn't want to be anyplace they couldn't take care of themselves and their belongings. She didn't like the dirty place no matter how elegant the sculpture and architecture under the grime.

At the conference, he kept distant from people, yet on the last day, when he had to leave, he felt choked up, unable to speak, teary-eyed. He left the building quickly and returned to the hotel.

He and his wife moved on to Finland. Crossing high

above the Baltic Sea, he saw the white-tipped waves like stars in the night sky of the dark waters.

He wanted to go to St. Petersburg in Russia, close to the border of Finland, but was advised against it because of the expense and the danger. He wanted to see the Hermitage and other museums, if there were any. But he could be robbed.

But what is faith if not a challenge of desire? he thought.

His wife had said she wanted to go to St. Petersburg, but now she changed her mind. She wasn't sure about going to Russia. It would cost money, the visa, the ticket, the hotel, the meals. He heard the mafia, who were the former KGB officers, stole whatever they could from tourists. The communist regime had controlled corruption. Now that control was gone. Anything could happen. He stayed in Finland in the hotel and felt a sadness grip his whole being. He didn't know, but the land knew; it was anger at himself.

He and his wife could coexist, he thought as they toured museums, though when they traveled, she wore on him, and he on her without their separate studies to withdraw into; both looking forward to the return when he could retreat into his space and she into hers.

Back in Minnesota, the late October afternoon was cold and overcast. At the Manor, he saw his mother was desperately ill and near death. They sat around her bed. His father was in a chair by her side, openly weeping at times. His wife comforted his father.

He told his father he missed the neighborhood churches when he was in Europe. America was full of churches. He was trying to make conversation. There was a church on every corner in America. Unlike the large cathedrals in Europe.

The doctor and his father decided not to move his mother to the hospital, but let her die in the room she shared with her husband. It would be too hard to take him back and forth to be with her. There was nothing the hospital could do. It only would be an unnecessary cost.

For several nights he waited at the Manor until the last minute, then drove back to Morris, went to classes, read papers, graded them, held office hours, returned to the Manor, and sat with his father and mother through the night. The doctor didn't know how long she would last. There was no sound coming from her except an occasional moan, and then even that stopped. Her eyes were glazed when the nurse looked under her eyelids.

"Is she in pain?"

"No. We're giving her morphine," the nurse said.

Morphine? His mother, gentle as a rose, hooked on the thorn of morphine?

In her casket, his mother was breathing. He could see it from where he sat. He still thought of her in terms of someone who would fix him something.

A minister read from Matthew 8:11. *"And I say that many will come from the east and west, and sit down with Abraham, and Isaac, and Jacob, in the kingdom of heaven."*

Then his father spoke. His wife was in the bosom of Abraham, his father said.

He had been asked if he wanted to say something about his mother, but he declined.

The early snow and sleet fell against the window in the Lutheran church on Second Street off Main, where his father had preached. It seemed to him the land also said his mother was in Abraham's bosom.

After the service, he rode in the line of four cars through the inclement weather. Most of the old congregation offered their regrets at the door of the church. They wouldn't go to the cemetery. It was the weather.

In the cemetery, the men pulled the casket from the hearse. His father walked between him and his wife behind the pall bearers. One man stumbled on the wet incline to the grave, letting go of his end of the casket. His father leapt forward as though he were a young man. He helped the man lift the casket again. His father guided it toward the open grave as the snow drove into his face. He and his wife tried to pull his father back between them, but he walked with the casket, the wind flopping their coats and the skirt of the platform where they placed the casket over the open grave.

After a few more words, the people hurried back to their cars to get out of the wind.

After they left, the earth swallowed her without chewing.

At the University of Minnesota at Morris, before the department meeting, they asked about the trip to the conference in Prague. In Finland, he'd been close to Russia, but the tour was canceled, he said. He'd seen enough poverty and hopelessness in Eastern Europe. Did he need to go to Russia?

Oh, and yes, they were sorry about his mother.

The snow continued to fall. He shoveled intermittently, thinking of buying a snowblower like his neighbors. But he would shovel the snow by hand. At least he had taken the piles of leaves to the city compost and covered the rosebush with a pile of leftover leaves. How could he live in a place so cold? he thought as he brought in wood for the fire. But he hadn't ever lived anyplace but Minnesota. He had walked through the snow to school six months of the year. He had sledded and ice skated until his feet felt like chunks of ice. He remembered ice fishing on Lake Osakis, and riding in a friend's truck on the frozen surface. The boys liked to skid their cars and trucks across the ice, though his parents warned him. He remembered the snowmen they made at church with names like Jeremiah, Ezekiel, and Habbakuk. He remembered a friend who died of exposure when he tried to walk to Osakis from his stalled car. Maybe he could live on the land because his mother had been severe and the land was like his mother.

His breath in the cold was an igloo. Or the tail of a comet. Or soda-water bubbles in *More Things Any Boy Can Make*.

Sometimes in the mornings, when he shaved, he saw half of his face covered with snow.

The University of Minnesota at Morris had been an Indian boarding school, and Indian students still attended without paying tuition. There were not many, maybe eighty out of nearly two thousand students, but once in a while he had one in his class. They didn't look like he thought they should. He didn't feel any particular kinship with them. They wrote about environmental poverty. They wrote about the land as themselves: blue oat grass, spike grass, big bluestem, ribbon grass, switchgrass, Indian grass, reed grass, moor grass, hair grass, sedges, bottlebrush, rushes, and the rest of the tallgrass prairie cleared for farmers' crops, just as they had been.

He felt the heaviness of their thoughts. The animals uprooted. Some of them pushed to extinction. The Indian students wrote, but they rarely talked in class.

In early November, not long after the funeral, his father took a turn for the worse. Maybe it was the result of his exertion at his wife's funeral. Maybe it was the emptiness of the room without her. His father talked to his dead wife as though she were in the room with him. Sometimes he preached. The armies of Sennacherib were camped outside the Manor.

He sat beside his father's bed on Saturday afternoon and listened to his father remember back through his life. His wife couldn't spend that much time at the Manor and would bring her own car and leave by herself. He listened to his father talk to his grandparents. He knew his father had been lost once, probably as a boy. He heard him calling for them. He knew his father had been disappointed in the ministry, not accomplishing what he wanted, watching his ideals wash away as he dealt with the frailties of his congregation and himself. He may have even been disappointed in God.

A small rock had hit the windshield of his car. He saw the crack in the corner as he left the Manor. He watched it travel the width of the glass as he drove Highway 28

49

between Morris and the Manor in the early winter. It was the warm air from the defrost on the inside, and the cold air that came early to Minnesota on the outside. It was the rough road that jarred the car between the two places.

Finally, he had to have his windshield replaced. But the insurance paid for it. His wife filled out the forms.

His car also needed repair again. From the window of the waiting room, he saw the rust on the door, and in the wheel wells. How ugly the car was. He worked on final grades for the fall quarter as he waited. The grimness of his life had the assurance of Calvin.

Maybe that was why he wanted to think about relativity. Maybe it was a reaction to his rigid life. He thought about the wheel that steered his car. The four wheels that moved his car over the road. One wheel was solid, the others filled with air. There was another wheel in his trunk. There were smaller wheels that turned inside his engine.

He liked similarities that were different. Such as cherub and *kur-rib*. Or even the name of Osakis. It was originally *O-Za-Te*, a fork in the trail, or *O-Zah-kees*, lake of the Sauk. It had also been called *O-Sau Ki-uk*.

He decided he could get used to uncertainties as long as his certainties held. He liked to think of the land as moving. He liked, especially, to think of time as relative.

He knew gravity warped light waves. What warped time? What if what seemed millions of years was not millions of years? How could time curve so that it looked longer the further back he looked? How could it curve, becoming elongated or magical as the tricks in his boy's book, mirrors at both ends of the box making it look like there were more soldiers?

He wanted to say, *the man who heard the land heard time*. But how could he reconcile the two parts of time he knew? The biblical and the scientific?

A black hole warped time.

He thought of the black hole. What was the dark matter? The dark energy? What could it do? What was in those vast open places of the universe?

He thought of God, the creator, who was only trying to play his hand, hoping everyone wouldn't move on without him. But God seemed stuck with six thousand years since the creation of Adam. But science pushed man back to millions of years. Sixty-five million? What exactly was it now?

It was Christmas and he had to stay in his wife's mother's house near Moorhead because of the cold. Usually, when they visited her family, he stood outside while her sisters talked, but now the windchills were unbearable.

In the entry hall, he saw the knit hat he had bought for his wife's niece in Prague. He wanted to ask her to play the piano. He could hear the land stir under its coat of snow. He heard the snow as a principle of transience that endured. It wasn't there all year, but it was there every year. He wanted to think about his thought as his niece played the piano, but there were too many people in the room talking—and now two of them were line dancing—and no one wanted to be quiet while she played.

He wanted to leave, but he had nothing to do except drive to the Manor and sit with his father, unless another blizzard came. He thought of being stuck at his wife's family's house. He thought how his niece had grown. He wanted to ask what she was doing in a family where she didn't fit, but he couldn't talk to her.

Nothing had been asked of him. He had not learned to give of himself. He had not been taught. He had received and not given. He was unconnected. He had only himself.

52

His father continued to preach his sermons in his room at the Manor. Through the rest of December. Into January as the winter quarter began and he faced new groups of students in his classes.

They stomped in out of the cold. The smell of the cold on their clothes lasting nearly through class. They waited outside his office or after class with questions. They left messages on his phone asking for changes in their last-quarter grades. How much like a balancing act was his teaching?

His father's sermons weren't complete sermons, but fractures of sermons he'd preached over the years. Sometimes he could remember the Sunday they came from.

It seemed it was always snowing. He had to scrape his windows every time he left the Manor. He hated the redundancy, the repetitions of his routines.

Each Saturday when he returned, his father thought he was still in the pulpit. He thought he was in his field. He thought his wife was in the kitchen and he was hungry.

Sometimes his father had to be restrained when he visited. The nurses told him his father had tried to leave the Manor.

One Saturday, he found his father in another room, a cold corner room with windows on two sides. They said he called his wife's name until they moved him to the end of the hall and closed his door.

He heard anger in his father's voice. Maybe it was only frustration. No, it was anger. He heard it clearly. His peaceable father was storming now. He felt a momentary fear of his father's anger. Hadn't he punished him once, doubling his belt and hitting his bare knees?

When he knew where he was, his father didn't want to be in the Manor. He didn't want to be at the end of his life. Why wasn't his wife there? Where was she? he asked. Sometimes he told his father she'd be back soon. Sometimes he told him he'd been to the cemetery. Then his father knew where he was and what had happened to her.

Sometimes he was coherent. They talked about scriptures. Other times he drifted back into his confusion. His wife didn't used to be late. What could have happened? He would not admit his anger to himself.

Then his father was back on Sennacherib encamped outside the Manor. He was afraid of the assault that was threatening him.

God would take care of him, he tried to assure his father. Sennacherib would not get into the Manor. Sennacherib was a reminder of the strength of opposition that could be overcome by faith.

The doctor thought his father's confusion might be caused by the medication. The doctor tried giving him smaller doses, and it helped somewhat.

Driving from the parking lot, he felt an aloneness he had never felt in his isolated life. He had had tenure with his parents and now he had none.

He drove past the Lutheran church on Second Street off Main. He drove past the old parsonage and stopped. Sitting for a moment in front of the house, he thought he felt time move. Great clouds crossed over the earth, and he moved with them. He thought of the time when he hadn't known change. But now, how quickly life passed. The more it moved on, the faster it went. When he was a boy, time had been slow. Everything also had been big. The house. The town. Men had once lived nine hundred years. Adam. Seth. Enoch. Now his father was dying at eighty-four.

In fact, he thought as he drove on, there had been no time when the Saturday matinee rolled before his eyes in the dark of the Empress Theater on Central Avenue. Central Avenue itself rolled into Lake Osakis at the end of the next block, where the wind rolled across the water and the sun slipped beneath the gray platform of the clouds.

Lake Osakis itself rolled under the sky like the old stage to Fort Abercrombie that kept the land open during the Dakota Conflict of 1862. He imagined Gumby and Pokey riding with the stage and the wind lassoing a boy who wanted to live as a boy forever, but was pulled into the awful reflective, self-absorbed life he was stuck in and couldn't get out of, even it he was free to teach and travel. And what was it the earth withheld from him anyway? What was the purpose of the mystery?

What was Abraham's bosom that would consume him too? He had one foot in its mouth already. He had not been rowdy. He had been good, he wanted to plead to the earth, but it was not enough. He was caught by the cannibal earth with bones in its nose, eating everyone, and now it had his father. He held his thoughts to himself like toys.

He remembered he had seen a grasshopper or a cricket struggling against something, its back legs dismembered. As he watched, he thought at first he saw thin antennae moving at the insect's mouth. He soon realized they were not part of the grasshopper. They were something different; something sinister. They were spider legs.

A small spider was inside the grasshopper's mouth, eating its brains. He found a hull in the corner of the room; a headless grasshopper, also with its back legs gone. First the spider must chew off the legs, then attack inside the mouth, leaving the insect a helpless victim to a slow and agonizing death. This was the nature that spoke to him? This was what he saw in his mother's neat house; a parsonage in which prayers were raised to God?

Had he not read articles about black holes? Wasn't there a possibility that the universe was eating other universes?

Was not something eating his father?

Gruesome land. Gruesome life. He wanted it to be quiet. He didn't want to see anything like that again. He didn't want to think about it again.

56   He remembered the Osakis creamery as he returned to the Manor on another Saturday. The malts he used to order. The Cyclone house built to withstand strong winds that sometimes swept the lake. The Osakis bait shop where tourists came to the resorts around the lake, bought minnows, crawlers, wax worms, and leeches.

He remembered Osakis history as a map of the land. It gave him pleasure to think how things had been. He liked to imagine the stage that traveled the military road between St. Paul and Fort Abercrombie on the Red River to say, THIS LAND IS OURS! YOU INDIANS, YOU WIND AND COLD, NOTHING CAN STOP US.

He had always liked to imagine the past. It was a repetition in his life that he liked.

He thought of glaciers melting, leaving ten thousand lakes in Minnesota. He thought of the forests and prairie grasses. The buffalo, deer, beavers, raccoons. He thought of Indians eight hundred years ago according to Osakis historical records. He recalled that the Dakota hunted and gathered roots and berries and planted corn and squash. They called the place *O-Za-Te*.

Then the Ojibwe wanted the rice beds on the shores of the lakes and they pushed the Dakota further west. They said, *O-Sau Ki-uk*.

Then the Sauk came. They said, *O-Zah-kees,* but did not stay.

In 1836, a French geographer named Nicollet wrote Osagis on the map. *O'-say-gus*. But in his memory, it always had been *Osakis, O'-say-kiss,* with some disagreement among those in Osakis as to the origin of the name.

He stood at the lake at the end of Central Avenue in the bitter cold, trying to pull his coat collar up around his ears. He remembered the men backing their boat trailers into the lake, where he heard them blame the cormorant for the smaller number of walleye in the lake each year. He remembered how his imagination fished the lake each time he came from the Empress of darkness in the movies. He remembered how he had thought himself twirling with the stars or the northern lights. He remembered when the boundaries of the land danced for him, skimming across the lake, easing known boundaries of shore and boat into lake and sky overhead.

How could there be such pain in his life? Where had that thought suddenly come from? What caused it? He had not served in war. He had not broken bones. His injuries were minimal. Sometimes he still felt a tenderness in his scalded foot. Maybe it was loss he felt. The erasure of what he was. How could God remove him from an Indian heritage that would have been meaningful, if that's what had happened? Place him on the ice field of Minnesota? How could he live on nothing? A frozen lake that would thaw and drown him? How could God put him in a quiet, enormous universe? A migration trail that wasn't?

He got into the car to get out of the cold. To get back to his duties, he thought of the weather of space. The environment of the sky. He thought of one part of space eating another part of space. He was trying to leap toward an understanding. A statement. He wanted to say, *the man who heard the land* heard.

His mother had had an eye for sin. She had questioned his going to matinees thinking it was against the will of God. And how could he, without God, put together this vast incomprehensible earth on which he lived his life?

He could think he was on the ocean crossing to Europe, far away from Osakis if he lifted his eyes just a moment above the lake and saw only the sky. He imagined a hand-crocheted lake for a passport stamp. Its waves unhooked from the shore. He remembered the women crocheting in church. *Crochet*. It was a word in which no *t* sounded. Probably the word had come with the French.

He felt the past swirling everywhere. In memory, things always seemed out of order. Pollution grew over the earth as man lost his first light and was doomed to his own darkness. Only JESUS could get him out. His father shouted his savior's name when he arrived in his room at the Manor.

He heard the nurse say if they couldn't calm his father, he would have a stroke. He tried to calm him. He talked his father through their memories, the way he went through the antique store in Moorhead. Or maybe if he recited the right name from the Bible, he could spark a quieter sermon in his father. Sometimes he read a Psalm to him.

He wept as he left the Manor that day, whatever day it was, whatever time he was in, his chest heaving, his whole body heaving, in a cry that was anger that his parents had kept him in a box. No, he cried because he had liked the box, and was now being forced out.

Euphrates, he thought. All around him, he felt the trees freighted with snow. He thought of winter rushing toward summer, summer rushing to fall again, winter rushing to deeper winter, which seemed to stand still a while.

He mentioned to the department head that he would like to be considered for a tenure-track position. The department head told him that all tenure-track vacancies had to be filled through a nationally advertised, competitive search.

The department head told him that he should publish a book if he was interested in tenure. But what would he publish? What interested him? A book on time shrinking? A book about the land? Surely the land had a voice. But how did it say what it said?

The new professor the English department hired had published articles that were announced in department meetings. The new professor began to hint that he wanted to go to conferences. The new professor wanted to teach a literature class on the environment, which would leave him with only composition.

That night he thought again about writing his book. He felt his position at Morris eroding. Did the land feel the same when its woods were cleared for fields? When its streams were polluted by industrial waste?

He thought about the land. The landscape was a testament of man's destructiveness. *Man is the cannibal*, he thought the land said.

He thought about time. Had there been other times

before Genesis? He knew there had to be. Or could there be times within time? He had always liked Genesis 6:4. *There were giants in the earth in those days.* Could that be during the time of the dinosaurs? But his father would never say what he thought the verse meant.

How could he reconcile the conflicts? His thoughts swam like snow over the road. Had there been a pocket, or pockets, of time when the animals were big? Birds were big. Time was big.

He started his book: ONCE THERE WAS TIME.

The history of time was not a linear mass, but an agent made shorter, quick as a bullet as it moved toward its end. The previous century had seemed huge with possibility. Now a new century had begun and another would follow it. The time spent in his boyhood was enormous. Now it grew smaller. Already he was rushing to turn in grades, to get his wife a birthday present, to meet his appointments. The beginning of class seemed large. He hurried to finish his lecture at the end. Soon, he'd spend Christmas again standing outside his wife's family's house in the cold.

Hadn't time also been relative in the Bible? He found the passage in the Bible he kept in his office. Even time had moved backward.

I will deliver you out of the hand of the king of Assyria; And this shall be a sign unto you from the lord, that the Lord will do what he has spoken: I will bring again the shadow of the degrees, which is gone down in the sun dial of Ahaz, ten degrees backward. So the sun returned ten degrees, by which degrees it was gone down. Isaiah 38:6-8.

That meant he would have to eat breakfast again. Walk through the snow. Find a parking place in the crowded university lot. Listen to his wife sneeze. They both had colds. His students were always coughing on him in the classroom. In the office.

He thought further about time. If he was late, time moved fast. If he was early, it was slow.

He felt an urge to look at the hair on his arm under a magnifying glass again.

Straight time was an illusion. It was a relativity like light and energy. Could he know the course of anything? His father was born at the beginning of a century when it seemed he had forever; now he was confined to bed and he had a matter of months at most. The century had seemed huge with possibility; but it had rushed to the pinhole of its end. Now another century opened into a large beginning.

What if time were something in his old book, *More Things Any Boy Can Make*? He could write about experiment with change. What if time was enormous for someone, while for him it rushed? Could time be both at the same time? Were there boys somewhere like him, who didn't know how time could change?

He remembered the fish trap he tried to invent as a boy, but had given up, though it still bothered him to see a hook in the mouth or swallowed by a fish. He wanted the catch to be painless for the fish.

In death, his father would be delivered from time. "Take my watch," he heard his father say as he stood by his bed in the Manor. He and his wife had given the watch to his father. He looked at it as his father spoke to someone he couldn't see.

"Are you going to church?" his father asked in a moment of clarity.

He had to look to make sure his father was talking to him. "Yes," he said, and his father seemed satisfied.

One day is with the Lord as a thousand years, and a thousand years as one day. II Peter 3:8

The cloning of time. He had wanted to think about the land, but time kept getting in the way. Time made itself. More and more of itself.

He sat in the office he shared with two other adjunct faculty members. But there was too much noise to think. Students kept bothering him. Other faculty members were talking about basketball in the next office. He already had memos and department forms to fill out about course schedules and book lists for the fall quarter. He always was the first to get his schedule done. He had calls to answer. Someone had turned on Minnesota

Public Radio. Someone else was using the computer and he couldn't work with the clicking keyboard. He decided to go home and work in his own study, leaving his phone number on the door.

LAND AND TIME WERE CONNECTED.

LAND WAS TIME.

TIME WAS LAND.

History was distorted and seemed far away when actually, it was not, and time speeded up and things got smaller rushing toward their end. And man who had been made in God's image, his father would say, chose his own way to think, fed on his own will, kicked against the walls of God, pushed God and his restraints aside and marched toward the fast finish of this game rushing toward its loss. The way the land was always there, yet rushed by, depending on the speed he drove.

THE LAND WAS IN ABRAHAM'S BOSOM.

What was he writing? Maybe he read too many articles in the *Scientific American*. He had to get a grip on himself.

He returned to his original sentence.

ONCE THERE WAS TIME.

One day and a thousand were the same. One year and a thousand were the same. One thousand and a million were the same. One million and a billion.

What if the warp of time caused other changes? What if time expanded and contracted? What if atmospheric pressures during those times made the earth different than it was in the beginning? What if the disruption of atmosphere changed the land and life upon the land? He liked to imagine the possibilities.

Think of the changes that extreme heat or cold could make.

After the big bang, as the earth began to cool, certain things became possible that had not been possible before. Gases could come together and form particles necessary for life.

His father only wanted to talk about the fall of man. The results of disobedience. Actually his father would say, the old disruption was caused by the fall of Satan and the warring angels. He even had a Bible verse for it. Luke 10:18. *I saw Satan as lightning fall from heaven.*

What if he felt a center in himself? What if the Indian woman had not given away her baby, but raised him in her own tradition? What if he were not tossed between all the possibilities? What if he were not made from a culture he was not?

There was a basketball game in Minneapolis. Some of the men in his department were going. There was another ticket. Did he want to go with them?

It was twelve below when they left Morris on a mid-January afternoon, but the forecast was clear. Already the moon stung the sky.

He wasn't used to the noise of all the voices. The arena was as loud as his parents' house had been quiet. The men got settled. The Wolves were behind eight, twelve, fourteen points. How his expectations, which had been high, were now dashed. Like everything else.

He watched the teams moving from one end of the floor to the other. Sometimes he just looked at the crowd. The Wolves rallied a few times during the game, and he cheered with the men, belonging to their ritual of competition.

When the men went for beer, he stayed in his seat. He didn't drink. His parents prohibited it. He had seen its effects—he remembered the Indians who wandered through Osakis. He wasn't going to be caught in that.

On their way back to Morris, the men talked about hunting and fishing. They talked about treaty rights.

It took plywood to build an ice-fishing house. Paint. Sometimes the houses froze to the ice and had to be pried loose.

He'd seen a lake full of cars. A car full of the lake. However he wanted to look at it.

Sometimes when he was driving, other places came to him. The Jacobson Building, 1932, next to the Empress Theater on Central Avenue where Foster Gamble's father worked. What had happened to Foster, and Jason, his brother?

He remembered when they played basketball, and raced their bicycles past the Pollard Mill and Elevator to the underpass on Lake and First Avenue West, to feel the roar of the train above them.

Hadn't he wanted to live in a boxcar when he was a boy? Unhooked from everything.

Maybe Foster and his brother were still boys. Maybe time had not changed for them.

When was it that Jason skidded off his sled and broke his arm? When was it that he had the twig jammed into his scalp? Time didn't seem a uniform track on which to move.

What would it be when all the snow melted in the spring? he heard one of the men say.

He knew the story of winter. First there was frost. Then a thin sheet of ice on the lake. Then ice thick enough the fishermen drilled for water with their augers. Then they'd drive their trucks across the ice with their rods and jigging sticks, their Coleman stoves and rattle reels, their benches, kettles, and blankets.

As the lake froze, the ice expanded. Often he had heard the ice pop as it pushed and broke over itself. The ice talked, stuttering the old tongues of a primitive language.

Osakis.

Osagis.

O-Zah-Te.

O-Zah-kees.

O-Sau Ki-uk.

Now the men talked about their snowmobiles. He knew there were twenty thousand machines in Minnesota looking for places to go, chewing up the roads with their studs, leaving their claw marks on the pavement, their petroglyphs of metal traction, from Morris to Osakis to Moorhead.

The driver was going too fast. He knew it. And he would be last to be let out of the car.

On a curve outside Morris, the car nearly slid off the road. He kept bumping into the man next to him as the car swerved. The driver should be careful of the patches of black ice. He sat in the dark of the car not saying anything.

When he got out of the car to let another man out, his foot broke through the hard crust of snow along the side of the road. He felt the cold that stung as if it were the hot water he remembered rushing into his shoes when his heater coil broke.

They let another man off at his house and another, and finally it was his turn to get out of the car and go into his house and sit in his study and listen to the ringing in his ears from the noisy arena, and realize the evening was over. He even thought, once, he heard a note from the piano in the living room no one played.

There were tire tracks through the ice under the snow by his drive. He had to get to a department meeting and classes. He backed from the garage and got caught crosswise in the grooves. He rocked the car back and forth. He chopped at the ice ridges, but they were solid. He wouldn't ask his neighbors. None came to help. His wife was suddenly behind the car. He could have hit her if the car had jerked backward over the ice. She stood there until he waved her back in the house. Then he went in the house. He called AAA. He was on the phone three, seven, eleven minutes. His wife brought him the newspaper to read, but he had looked through it at breakfast. He motioned for her to bring his briefcase full of students' papers. She looked impatient. She needed to call her office. She would be late. He was going to take her because of the icy roads. She fretted in the kitchen. Its clean surfaces skidded his eyes back into himself. The pans and dishes, washed, dried and on their shelves. The kitchen was as small as his mother's old kitchen had been enormous. A whale's belly, he remembered it.

Finally someone answered. He explained how he had tried to get his car out of the ice grooves in the street by his driveway. AAA explained they were behind because of the weather. It would be an hour or two. He would wait at his house, he said. Yes, he had a membership. It was a gift each year from his parents. Now he would have to renew it himself.

His wife called her office, and he called school and said he would miss the department meeting. He would be late for his office hours. His classes were still several hours away. He would be there for his classes.

The tow truck pushed him over the ruts and into the street. He signed the receipt and the truck drove off. He chopped at the ice until his wife came out of the house, then drove up the street on his way to take his wife to work, and then to the office, wondering what had been decided in the department meeting without him.

There was an environmental conference in Washington, D.C. His department head asked him to go. The new professor had a conflict with another conference and couldn't attend.

How would the trip be funded? he asked.

The usual way. The university would cover half.

Would the university pay for the entire trip if the new professor was going? he wanted to ask. Were they paying for the trip the new professor was taking? But he didn't ask.

He talked to his wife about the conference as they ate at home that night. She had made a stew and he had bought some bread at the bakery.

They decided he should go if it would help him write the book he wanted to write.

He arrived at National Airport on the Potomac. He saw the smokestacks across the river, the white sail of a boat on the river. If only all the snow in Minnesota would shrivel to that. The windless air. The roar of the planes as they took off and landed. Small in the distance, in inverse proportion to time, which got bigger the farther away it was.

He saw the monuments of Washington, D.C. Jefferson. Washington. Lincoln. He saw the Capitol dome. He watched the government buildings from the cab. Bureaucratic architecture. Clean. Gray. Utilitarian. The museums. Granite or marble. No buildings in Washington, D.C., were over nine stories, to maintain the view of the monuments.

He thought of the architecture of time. It was a triangle overturned. Growing smaller toward its point. He opened his notebook and made a note.

Then he wrote:

Multum in Parvo.

Freight trees.

Barges.

River traffic.

Why had he come all that way when there were probably not fifteen people to hear him? There were many concurrent panels at the large, international conference where English was the approved language, yet he heard many languages.

How ugly the woman's laugh was. He sat by himself in the crowd waiting to hear the speaker. Why were they all there to see this speaker? Why didn't he have anything to say that would make a crowd fill a room?

The woman's voice wheezed by him. He could almost feel it brush his hair. He wanted to turn to her and twist shut her mouth on her face.

Why did she think he wanted to be part of her life? To hear the information on her activities. Her opinions. Her air that was killing the trees.

He was writing in his notebook. ICE JAM. ICE DAM. There was a slight stain on their bedroom ceiling. He saw it before he left Minnesota. He would have to call someone to steam and shovel the snow from his roof in Minnesota when he returned. Did he still have the number from several years ago? It had been a while since the snow had been that deep. He was sure his wife had the phone number. He drew the ice dam in his notebook. The slope of his roof was under several feet of snow. The heat rising from the warm house into the attic found cracks and light fixtures and vents and chimney flues and hatches. The heated air warmed the underside of the roof. The snow next to the roof melted. The melted snow froze at the cold edge of the roof, causing the ice dam. The melted snow behind the dam backed up through the shingles and leaked into the insulation and plaster. The siding. He imagined the expense.

The conference was overwhelming. He had to get away. He walked through the Rotunda at the Capitol. He didn't want to take a tour, but just pass through. He saw the word *country*. What was land to the government? It was an idea, a state of mind, not an actual space. A constitutional system of checks and balances written before the leaders even knew what land they had.

What had the land said then? When it was unknown?

He thought of the term he heard at the conference, *cognitive geography*. Land is what you think it is. But land to him was not defined by the human mind. The human mind was more defined by land. Wasn't the lack of land one of the reasons conquerors and dictators had gone to war?

Next, he walked to Union Station and asked how to get to the National Geographic Society on the Metro. At the Farragut exit, he surfaced on the long escalator. The Geographic Society was across the street from the National Mining Association, a black cubelike building, the same shape of downtown Washington, D.C., buildings. They were all glass or stone cubes along the street.

This was why he was in Washington, D.C. To walk through the bright covers of the *National Geographic* magazines. To be with the words *geography, topography, atlas, map*. They were words that tilled his imagination. He remembered looking at the magazines at his friend's house in Osakis when he was a boy.

He went through an exhibition in Explorer's Hall: the Shackleton Antarctic Expedition. In 1914, Shackleton entered the Weddell Sea in his ship, the *Endurance*. But the ship had caught in the ice as the sea froze, and the *Endurance* had broken apart, had been squeezed apart, and shattered into kindling. He stood looking at the artifacts, photographs, and film. The expedition was stranded for ten months on the ice, surviving on penguin meat and seal. When the ice floes began to break up, Shackleton and a few of his men rowed the lifeboat back to Elephant Island, promising to return for the rest of the men. But storms prevented his return for nearly a year. When Shackleton finally got through, he found his men alive. All of them survived. He had to suck back tears as he saw the photographs of the brave men with ice in their beards. As he saw the actual lifeboat and the film of the rolling sea in the last room. He walked by the glass cases again. He saw the Bible carried by the ship's second officer. The eye goggles and navigational tools.

We had pierced the veneer of outside things . . . we had seen God . . . [we had] heard the text that nature renders. Sir Ernest Shackleton.

Outside, the evening sun was a *National Geographic* yellow.

Back in Minnesota, the roofing company did not find an ice dam. The stain on the bedroom ceiling was an oddity that shouldn't cause alarm.

That night, from the window in his study, he saw the blind, fish-eyed moon beyond the cold roof of his house. It reverberated with the snow-covered land. Sometimes he felt the cold would never leave.

He said, *frozen moon. Bucket of road salt.*

He thought he could hear the white sound of the moon, but decided it was only the static on his wife's radio she left off-station to sleep. Or maybe it was the painting of Sennacherib in his attic.

Yawning moon. Milk-eyed moon. Cyclops moon. In a

few days it would be a half-closed eye. The moon unreliable, yes, but always there. Most always there.

A snowman's decapitated head. A marble rolling across the sky. Heel-print moon. Sledgehammer moon cracking white rock. Rolling moon. Roaming moon.

He worked with his words, thinking what he could write. No wonder no one else went to the conferences. It took his concentration from what he should be doing. Yet, at the same time, it gave him ideas. He often struggled with them before the students in his classes that moved in such fast succession he sometimes felt he couldn't keep up.

Was he like the moon, a lesser light, between his parents who were the earth and sun for him?

On Saturday, before he drove to the Manor, he sprinkled through his small collection of foreign coins, which reminded him of waves on Lake Osakis. He had washed them until they shined.

He could have spent a year's salary on the fourteenth-century German deer candlestick and lived off his wife. She liked to reconcile the accounts. Give her this one to work into their budget. But he hadn't.

Earlier that morning, he tried to concentrate on a student's paper. The health of an ecological system was its diversity. *Tell me something more*, he wrote on the paper.

He felt his old car struggle as he drove with his wife on Highway 28 along Lake Minnewaska to the Manor. Would the earth break down like a car? he thought.

His car wanted to die. When they reached the stop sign on Nokomis at Central in Osakis, he turned off the heater as he stopped. He needed a new car, but his adjunct professor's salary wouldn't allow it. His wife also worried about downsizing in the small company where she worked.

At the Manor, he held his wife's arm as they walked across the ice on the parking lot. The snow got into his shoes again. There were piles of snow in front of the Manor. In front of his house. In his drive. Across the sidewalks. On his roof. In his way. He remembered the Shackleton exhibit in Washington, D.C.

His mother would fret when he didn't wear galoshes or thermal boots; but the land made magicians and mothers disappear.

When they returned to Morris they stopped at Don's Restaurant, where he ate his pumpkin pie and had a bite of the apple and pear compote his wife had ordered. Once his mother made a lamb cake without coconut icing.

Now he thought of the stars as crumbs. Listen. Outside the restaurant, he thought he heard a piece of the moon. The whole night stopping there like an I-94 truck stop in space.

He watched the clouds roll across the moon. It seemed like the clouds were still, and it was the moon that was moving—the moon and the pines he stood under. He watched until his wife asked him what was wrong. He stopped staring into the sky, turned to her, and without saying anything, got into the car as though he had not been lost in thought in the parking lot at Don's Restaurant.

That evening when his wife was on the phone with one of her sisters, he read a book he bought in Finland.

He soon closed the book and sat in his study. He thought how rough life was in most of the world. If he prayed, would he be as blind as his father to everything that wasn't the Bible? He prayed to God: help me. He felt the downfall of the earth's timber, the rivers dammed and the levees made so steep in one place in India, the elephants couldn't drink. One fell down the steep incline and drowned. The earth was paved and shrink-wrapped. Time had to be shortened because otherwise it would be too long. He opened the book he was trying to write. *The land before time*, he wanted to write. *When no one could walk to where they had to go.* But that didn't make sense. He was not going to say something no one would understand, as he often did.

Instead he wrote, WE ARE ROBBING THE EARTH, then decided it was too blunt. How else could he say it? How else could he dig it out of his head?

He felt he was working on an eighth-grade science project, his father standing over him so he didn't violate the principles of God in the Bible.

How could he get any writing done? His Saturdays were cut into sections of grading papers, visiting his father, shoveling snow, having dinner with his wife, preparing for classes, reading. At least he wasn't interrupted by students coming into his office to talk about one matter or another.

Whenever he did get a chance to write, he felt he could fall into his writing without stopping and drown. THE EARTH, THE EARTHQUAKE, THE TIDAL WAVE, THE SNOWMOBILE STUDS, THE MOTORBOATS CHEWING UP THE LAKE IN SUMMER. He felt his old fear. There was something he didn't have. Something he needed. What was it he missed?

Between the water and the air was a layer of ice, which was a hard shelf between them. It was called the mystery of isolation. He'd known it all his life. It was a ticket to his thoughts of snowshoes, snow shovels, the deep freeze that was the Minnesota winter. Six months of heavy winter. Late October to mid-April, sometimes later.

One Sunday, in February, he drove through the snow to his office. At least he could find a closer place to park. He was going to grade papers and sit in the library and read.

The new professor was in his office. The door was open.

The new professor came out in the hall to talk to him, but he continued walking. "I was thinking about course offerings next fall. I want to teach the course on the environment you teach now," the new professor said, following him. "You don't mind—?"

"I do mind," he said, still walking. "That's the course I started. I've taught it for four years. I've already scheduled it. Why would I want to give it up?"

"I'm full time. I think I have precedence. There's still time to change course schedules."

"I've been here longer." He opened the door of his office, went in, and closed the door behind him. The new professor was not going to be deterred. He knocked on the door. In a moment, he opened the door.

"Maybe we should get something straight. I've been hired on tenure track. I plan to establish my area."

"Just so it isn't my area you establish." He was amazed at himself. He was standing up to the new professor. He didn't want to talk to him. He had papers to grade. He wanted to go to the library. He didn't like to feel threatened. He was not experienced at holding his own. He looked at his watch. "I have a lot to do. We can talk later."

When the new professor left, he sat in his office. He tried to read the papers while a snowplow rumbled across the sidewalks. He had thirty-five to grade in one course. One Indian student wrote about a ball in a box that was the moon. It held his attention for a moment. But all he could feel were his feet. His feet must have been frostbitten when he was a boy. They always were as cold as the weather.

He put aside the papers that he had to grade and went to the library. He read an article in the *Scientific*

American. He looked through a physics book, and thought about the book he would write, *A Boy Things Could Make*.

There was a place where a compass didn't work because of static electricity. Was it the dryness of cold? The dry ice? It was why snow swirled and the lake extended into the sky.

Was all his thinking, all his writing, nothing more than boys' games? No, he was working toward an understanding. The universe was governed by mathematical laws. Those laws governed what he experienced. Somewhere there was a complete theory of the universe. They just hadn't recognized it yet. There was an order physicists could partially understand. But what if they couldn't find the complete theory, or recognize it if they did? He was outside the mainstream, but he had read Stephen Hawking's *Black Holes and Baby Universes*, or tried to read it. He had read Galileo and Newton. He could think about those laws too. Even black holes were not completely black, but sent out radiation.

He still worried about the ice dam he thought was on the roof of his house. He thought about the unlit moon. He felt like he didn't want to do anything. Ever again. He was at the bottom of winter when it was at its lowest and he wondered whether he would survive.

He had a thought. Was it the land's or his own? Was that how the land spoke? Had it a tongue inside its head? Or did it share the tongue in his own mouth? Once in a while, if it lectured with a clear day, it would receive attention. Once in a while, it received praise. But often, it was ignored, or was the butt of complaint, or not considered in curricular development and departmental shifts.

A farmer would plow up the field, and in the night, when the animals roamed like dreams, they all felt their jobs, houses, families threatened.

The earth like time was going to turn over, shift, and everyone would know it. It had held still long enough. Now it would show them what it could do.

As he worked on his book he could feel the wheels turn, not the back tires, but the two front ones that turned the car in another direction. He was the important one to his parents, the whole universe had extended itself for him when he was a boy, but now he was the moon, a lightless ball as distant from the earth as the knowledge of the mathematical formula for the universe.

On his next visit to the Manor, he noticed his father wore a diaper. His father continued to drift in and out of memory. He didn't recognize his own son sometimes. Or his son was someone in his congregation and he had to speak to him about something, even if incomprehensibly.

He continued to drive back and forth between Morris and Osakis, usually now without his wife. There were days he didn't know what he was doing. There were days he entered his classes hardly knowing what he would say. He wanted to say to his father, go, the way his father had told him to leave for school the mornings he didn't want to go from his mother's warm kitchen into the cold, dark morning. It would be all right. Just go—. Whatever he faced was rugged. It would never be any other way. Yet there was a day when his reward was coming. Well, his father could step up to his reward.

Why was his father holding back? He knew he was going to die. He had preached the heaven he was going to all his life. His wife was there waiting. His God. The parents and grandparents he spoke to in his confusion in the Manor.

He sat dully at his father's bed as people shuffled past the door.

The earth hurt. It was inseparable from him. It was inconsolable. Immovable. It held him down.

He heard a piano down the hall at the Manor. He thought it sounded like the land.

What happened to his niece who played the piano? He'd have to ask his wife when he got back to Morris.

He stayed longer in his father's room. His father's heartbeat slowed and the nurses were concerned.

It was after dark when he left the Manor. As he returned to Morris on Highway 28 near Lake Minnewaska, the car slid off the road as if a hand pushed it. It was too far down in the ravine for anyone to see. The taillights blinked as he climbed to the highway, slipping on the ice. How many years had his parents warned him about the land and the cold? He could not survive if he was caught unprepared. At least he had on his down-filled coat with its hood, and his thermal boots and gloves. But he had no blanket in his car, nor a flare.

No one came along the stretch of road. He didn't know what time it was. Maybe around midnight. He knew he had to get out of the cold. He left the highway and walked onto the lake. He listened to the crunch of his footsteps as he walked over the ice. He didn't know how cold it was. The sting of the air in his nose told him it was at least ten below. In the moonlight, he could see several ice-fishing houses. He headed toward them. The first few were locked. He called out, but no one answered. His voice returned to him empty when he called again. He didn't want to make another noise because the emptiness frightened him. He didn't want to call out because the emptiness would know where he was.

He was probably alone on the lake, but sometimes a fisherman slept on the lake at night. He could hear his own breath as he searched for an open door. He could feel the cold already in his feet. Finally, he found an open house. He felt inside for the bench. Somewhere in the middle of the ice-fishing house that was the size of the storage closet in his garage was a hole he had to be careful of. He found a tarp he pulled over him, but it was as cold as the ice. He felt his exhaustion. He shivered. He felt the lake was a large mouth that would gulp him. It was sending up its hook for him and he deserved it. His parents raised him, yet he wasn't as grateful as he should be. He had never had a desire to know the mother who had given him birth. Or the father. The parents who adopted him had tried to make him into themselves without any thought of what he was or where he had come from.

Despite his fear, he got up and called out again. He knew there had to be someone sleeping on the lake all night. But there was no answer, not even a drunk ice fisherman. He again thought of the hole in the center of the ice-fishing house. It was the circle of a dark moon. What if he fell into it? He could feel the water wrapping him like a fish. Carefully, on his hands and knees, he felt for the bench.

He curled into a ball on the bench, trying to wrap the stiff tarp around him. Someone would find him before it was too late. He could think he was in church with his father preaching. His shivering made him feel like he was still riding in the car. Could he be in church if he thought he was? Or in his car driving away from the cold? Was it the same? The floor in church was always cold. He remembered his cold feet as he listened to his father.

Inside the ice-fishing house, the cold ate chunks of the walls until there was nothing between him and the cold, clear sky. Even in his house in Morris, he heard noises in the night. The ice on the roof creaked and talked in its sleep, making the house sound like a ship on the sea. But the ice-fishing house was a drifting raft.

As a boy, he had stayed on Lake Osakis one night with a friend and his father. It scared him when the ice jammed the lake. It scared him when he heard the voices of the land. They said he was a stranger to it.

Once he'd been in a plane far above the ocean. He imagined himself still far above the earth.

He had an impulse to leave the ice-fishing house. Shouldn't he keep moving? He thought once he heard a car. But his LOGIC told him to stay where he was.

The cold was a tribe that camped in Minnesota. He could hear the invisible ones talk on the lake. He knew they were there. His Indian students had mentioned the spirits. Nanabouju? Was that it? Wasn't there a possibility they were part of his heritage too?

Once he had gone to a powwow past Moorhead, in North Dakota. He was afraid. He belonged there no more than he belonged in the pulpit of his father's church. If he had Indian heritage, he didn't feel it at the powwow.

He was not fighting to have Indian heritage. He was neither Indian nor white. He probably was both. He was a blend of heritages. Dislocated. Out of place. He had no tribal footing. He was a general Indian. A general white. A mixed-blood who became an academic. Who was trying to become an academic. What did he have to hold onto?

But if he gave up in the ice-fishing house, there would be a deep sleep that slid over him from the ice and snow. He would see his mother and grandfather and great-grandfather, both blood and adopted. If he died, he would reach back and yank his father from the earth.

The cold was trouble like children. He heard the uprising of Sennacherib on the frozen lake that night. No wonder his father was afraid at the Manor. He had to think to keep his head in the ice-fishing house.

He thought of history moving backward. A train. A wagon. Cowboys and horses from his old bedspread. Another world he had known was there. What did it want? Why did it haunt him? What was he supposed to do? Just know it was there? Just be a witness? The earth plummeted across the sky. The ancestors, the extinct ones, were singing with the wind, some off-key. It was a rugged trip around the sun. He was there for the ride. And why was he there? To worship his maker, his father would say. No matter what. He should think of his blessings. He didn't have to pay for his father's keep in the Manor. He had his bases covered. He could think about writing a book in which he could say any absurd thing he wanted. Wasn't that the history of man? From the old pages of Job came the call to life in spite of circumstances, in spite of hopelessness or powerlessness. He could breathe. He had a drawer full of menthol cough drops in his office if he got a sore throat. He thought of the pair of gloves he also kept in the drawer, in case he lost the ones he wore to school. He thought of the wool scarf and a sweater hanging behind his door. He had had his food set in front of him all his life. He had time to think of the risks.

The relays. The overland stage at a time of Indian uprising. The savages on bicycles. He knew them. Felt them. The Bible said, *a man must be born again.* He'd accepted Jesus as a child. His father had seen to it. He had been a shepherd in the Christmas play when he'd wanted to be Joseph.

The earth was as alone as he was in the ice-fishing house, but it didn't help him feel one with the land. He often felt the land was more of a departmental meeting and he had no authority. He had felt distance from the animals also. But he had seen an intelligence in the animals too. No one recognized them as who they were, except his Indian students. But the students could be cruel also, full of alcohol. Not concerned with stewardship of the land. The earth had lost its heritage too.

A whole world was going on that no one knew. The earth was a living being. The land and the animals were bypassed, rejected. They were walking on the shoulder of a road that would narrow as it moved toward a washout into a gully. That's how it felt to have one's ground replaced by fields and subdivisions and cities. He was one with the earth. Yet he had to dominate. He couldn't be subordinate. There was something in nature that was fierce. One animal preyed on another. The life force had to have life force to sustain it. He'd seen the awful dominance all his life. Did he want to be part of it? The hunt. The kill. The land itself stalked and attacked with its turbulent weather and the extremes in the elements.

All accumulated on a rubber band of time stretched from the beginning.

In the ice-fishing house it all seemed so wild, turbulent, threatening, roving. Even Scripture cards pinned to his bicycle whirred on the spokes of his memory.

He felt his book was going by and he wouldn't be able to catch it.

Once again, he remembered the Shackleton exhibit at the National Geographic Society in Washington, D.C. Some of the men had become disoriented in the isolation of the Antarctic. Some of them had gone nearly crazy on the ice. But all of them had survived.

Later, Shackleton had tried to reach the South Pole again. But died of a heart attack. Shackleton had not reached the desire of his search, but his leadership and care of his men had been his destination.

He thought of the spurts and starts of his life. The disconnections. The frustrations. When had he cared for those around him? What was his story other than deflection from whatever had been? His heritage was subverted. Something that had meaning had been kept from him. Something that had no meaning had been given him. Well, let them keep it. For what good it did them.

He was tired of the mumbling earth. Why didn't it say what it thought? Clearly. He knew he was standing in the ice-fishing house, beating the walls. Thrashing against them. How often he felt he was in a car but someone else was driving. And what was wrong with that? It was the anger that kept him warm enough to survive. A heritage pasted on him. A hopeless impasse.

In the morning, the highway patrolman pushed open the door of the ice-fishing house and found him dazed. Maybe closer to half-conscious. He couldn't open his eyes in the light that flooded the door of the ice-fishing house. The patrolman said they found his car in the ditch and followed his footsteps across the lake. He should have stayed in his car. His frantic wife was in the patrol car. An emergency vehicle was arriving from Osakis. Soon he was inside the vehicle, rushing east into the light.

There was a message in the earth. Underneath what was seen and heard, another world moved. He had heard the trees, the fields and lake. They had language just as the birds who spoke to one another, and heard noises he didn't. The language of the land didn't sound like his language, but it was a language. It carried the knowledge of the animals, the history of the earth, the future, the light and dark, the stars and wheat. It was in the ball of his head he brought with him from space. This suitcase. This life.

"What if you lose your feet?" he heard his wife say. He must have been daydreaming. Now he realized he was in the hospital. He looked toward his feet, but saw only the covers. Why didn't he feel pain if he were in danger of losing his feet? Maybe the doctor had given him medication. He wanted to say something, but nothing came. He must have dozed off again. He realized his wife was still beside his bed when he felt her stir. A doctor stood beside them.

A toe on his right foot had to be amputated.

His wife covered her face. "But not the feet?" she asked.

"No."

His wife cried with relief.

The doctor continued talking, but he was lost in his thoughts again. He remembered when he was a boy, sleeping on the cot in the kitchen while someone had his room. Someone who had nowhere to go, or no one to turn to for help. He remembered a woman and a small child for several days, and a family with several children. He felt out of place in a place he was supposed to be, yet there had been some sort of comfort in the darkness of the kitchen.

"Do you want anything?" his wife asked.

He looked at her.

"More medication?" she took his hand.

"What do you want?" he asked his wife as she wiped her eyes.

"Order," she answered. "I want to have my hot pad in my hand and cook your supper."

"I didn't think you liked to cook," he said, and she cried again.

After surgery, he stayed in the hospital for two days while his feet began to heal. The doctor watched the other toes for the effects of frostbite, but it looked like none of the others would have to be removed. His fingers would be all right too.

A few of his classes were canceled, then a few of the professors took his classes for him. They came once or twice to visit. They brought reports of his classes. One brought him papers to grade.

He spent the cold, overcast days at the end of the winter quarter learning to walk while his feet were healing.

Standing at his bookcase, he opened the Finnish book again, but only felt the dark, cold Minnesota night that lasted a thousand years.

His students watched him hobble into class on crutches. They watched him wince if someone came too near. They watched his hands shake when he took roll. They listened to his crutches fall from the table or bang against the wall. They listened to his opening comments and the questions he presented, wanting the class discussions to begin.

It was now early March.

The hospital wouldn't take his father. The Manor didn't know what to do. Put him out beside the highway. Let the Lutheran church pick him up.

His father was sick. He sat by his father's bed as his father retched. He thought of the story the Indian student wrote in a paper last quarter. His father was too weak to protest a story that wasn't from the Bible.

When his father was quiet, he told him the story of a bright ball of light in a box in a hut.

A bird wanted it.

The bird became a berry, which the fisherman's daughter ate. The daughter became pregnant from the seed of the berry. Later, the bird was born as a child who cried for the bright ball in the box.

When the fisherman opened the box for the child, there was another box and another and another, and finally the last box was opened and the child had the bright ball. Then the child cried for the smokehole to be opened.

When the fisherman opened it, the child changed into a bird and flew through the smokehole with the bright ball in its beak. It placed the ball, which of course, was the moon, in the sky.

His father didn't say anything. He felt ridiculous for telling him the story. He tried to interpret for his father, how things are transformed into something else, born of another kind, in another place, only to return to the sky.

His father was the moon in the box.

The bird was the faith that would return his father to the sky.

He had read the papers of his Indian students. He knew how their stories had variable meanings. Of course, the students wouldn't think of the bird as faith. Or would they? At least they would understand how his transformation of the meaning could work.

The new Lutheran minister visited his father, but didn't stay long. And when the minister left, he put his hands on his father and said, *fly*.

One evening, he built a fire, then felt like working on his book while his wife played cards with some of her friends.

ABRAHAM'S BOSOM WAS BIG. ABRAHAM'S BOSOM WAS THE LAND THAT HELD THE TREES, THE WIND, THE DEER, THE BATS.

But what was he writing? He was rambling. His father had plowed the soil of his sermons as though they were fields. The new professor was probably in his study finishing an article that would be published in the *New Yorker* or *Scientific American* the next week. The editors were probably sitting up all night waiting for him to fax it, while he sat in his study stuck in Abraham's bosom. He fuddled his papers, paced the floor, and finally watched television. He was angry with himself. He felt an agitation in his legs. He got up, snapped off the television, looked at the moon from his window. He remembered the ice-fishing house, and shivered with fear. But it had been an Abraham's bosom. He had stayed in it and survived. He decided to put the book out of his mind for the evening, come back to it when he was fresh. He turned on the program again.

That night he dreamed of a boat dredging Lake Osakis. Parts of history turned up in the churning waters.

Maybe he would teach a history and literature course when the new professor took his environmental course.

Far, far back. Eight thousand years. Two thousand years before God created Adam. Had it only been six thousand years since the beginning of Genesis? How could the discrepancies exist? How could he make sense of them? How could he work with two fields of knowledge? Could they be reconciled? How could he get across the clunks? Where had that word come from? It's what he felt in his head. Clunk. Far, far back. Two thousand years before God created Adam, there were primitive game hunters. Then a Viking ship. As a boy, he heard that Vikings had been in Minnesota: the Kensington Runestone proved it, though his mother said the stone was a hoax. As a boy he liked to imagine the Viking ship on Lake Osakis. How did it get there? He didn't worry about it then or now. Maybe the Vikings had pulled it overland between the lakes. There were French voyageurs who carted their canoes and baggage, even their words, overland. Or maybe there had been more lakes connected by channels of water.

Maybe, like the voyageurs, he would have to keep pulling the weight of what he felt. Maybe he always would be without resolve. Wasn't that the way life was?

In the morning, he remembered his Osakis history book. He found it on the shelf and read through it while his wife cooked his breakfast.

In 1857, Mary Gordon had recorded the first settlement called Didier Corner, which became a stage stop on the military road from St. Paul to Fort Abercrombie on the Red River at the South Dakota border.

Then came a blacksmith, a store, a church, a school.

Maybe his book would develop like Osakis—one part at a time.

John Potter was another early name.

Donald Stevenson took over the Potter claim. Stevenson's gristmill produced O-Sa-Kiss flour, or maybe that was later.

Then his father had come to Osakis to be a minister.

And then he was a boy riding the bus to school, and riding his bike to the underpass. And then he was a man in front of students at the Morris campus.

He still felt the history buried in the land. In the lake. There was more than anyone knew. He thought about history as he ate breakfast with his wife.

He sat listening to the students as they struggled with issues in class discussion. He listened to the need for economic development as well as land preservation. The varying definitions of the responsible use of resources. The romanticization of nature, yet the harsh realities of it. The land as something to subdue; the land as part of oneself. Before he knew it, the class was over. How quickly the changes came. He would put his foot on time. If time had a brake.

"Literature is environment," he said to his class at the beginning of the spring quarter in late March. It was called spring, though it was twenty degrees. Snow, high as a house, was still plowed to the corners of the parking lots. "Literature is a restricted environment, but it simulates every environment."

The students looked at him.

"Define environment," he said and got answers of landscape or the atmosphere in which someone lived.

"Think of environment as literature," he suggested. "The interdependency of plot and character and theme— the interdependency of air and trees and water."

He was trying to jump-start the discussion in a class he was losing. He was sinking with it. How could he talk when he felt threatened?

"You can see that literature is like a tree with a vascular structure. You can see that literature creates environment."

His students looked at him.

"Or that environment creates literature. Or that literature is rooted in the environment," he said. "In the theory called *ecocriticism.*"

He wasn't always interested in answers, but in generating further questions, in showing students their options.

Osakis was partly in Douglas County, partly in Todd County. He liked a place that straddled counties. Had its feet in both, not knowing which to claim.

He liked some uncertainties, including even the threat of a job-share program at his wife's company, which upset her. She didn't want to share her job. Now she also knew how it felt to be threatened. She talked at breakfast while he watched the snow fall in their yard and thought of the shoveling he would have to do before he went to class. Her numbers were hers. And what would they do with less income?

He imagined he was Osakis standing with a foot in each county. Whichever side fell away, he would step to the side that stayed; when he could step without feeling the coldness and tenderness of his feet, even in his thermal socks.

It snowed through late March and into early April. How many blizzards had there been? Six? Eight? Freezing rain. Snow. Piles of it. Closing roads. Knocking down lines. Cutting off power. Filling the silence of the neighborhoods with sounds of snowblowers and generators. Tractors and snowplows. The stacks of cordwood in the backyards growing smaller, some almost gone.

The snow was his old toy, Gumby, bent in every way across roofs and trees. The snow was going to be the horse, Pokey, running all over when it melted.

After shoveling all weekend, he had to break loose from the schedule of the Manor and his classes. He wanted to drive to the antique store in Moorhead, northwest on I-94 on the North Dakota border. When they ate at the Atlantic Avenue Family Restaurant that night, he asked his wife if she wanted to visit her sisters and her mother. She decided that she did, if I-94 was opened and there wasn't another storm on the way.

The next day, he backed from his drive between mounds of snow higher than the car. They were cold, blue icebergs. The car slid on a patch of ice as if it were a ship when they started down the street.

Was Moorhead the old Fort Abercrombie? he thought on the way to Moorhead. His wife was quiet beside him in the front seat as he thought. He looked at the northern plains under the vast, open sky. The ice on ponds and marshes. The clumps of frozen sorrel weeds. The rolling land; the flatter fields. Battle Lake. Pelican Creek Wetlands. Otter Tail County. He knew the land was waiting under the white snow. No, in winter, he thought, the land was the snow. He saw a turquoise shed nearly the size of a barn. What must the land have been in its wilderness?

Sometimes he'd go to the Moorhead library. But he'd always ended up at the antique store. Could he still hear the stage arriving as he looked through the glass jars and farm implements and church pews? He could spend hours in the antique store. Time seemed not to move for him there.

In the store, he looked at the boxes of old fishing lures. He picked up a Brown's *Fisheretto*.

"Five brothers in the Brown family of Osakis made the wooden fish decoys and baits in the 1920s," the owner of the antique store said.

Maybe the lures were his father's. The ones he had given away without thinking. Why hadn't he paid attention?

There were other lures from Minnesota: *Finn Spoon*, *Heinkel's Special* made by the Gopher Bait Co. of Minneapolis, the *Scandahoovian Sockaroo*, all from the 1920s to the 1940s.

The antique store owner took a lure from another box. "LeRoy Chiovitte caught the biggest fish on record with a shiner minnow like this." He held it up. "Opening weekend of fishing 1979, a seventeen-pound, eight-ounce walleye—up north on the Seagull River near Grand Marais."

In the antique store, he saw a beaded pouch, a knife sheath, moccasins. He saw a heritage he could have been, should have been.

"Dakota," the man said, still following him along the counter.

It was the heritage he must have come from. But it was over. He was what the Christian evangelists and missionaries and white immigrants had wanted. His Indianness erased, he was like one of them.

Old ceremonies, whatever they were, were nothing to him. He held the beaded sheath in his hand. He recognized the workmanship, but it meant nothing. His new ceremony was the world that came. He belonged to the tribe of Christ who had come to the earth as the untenured. Powerless to the point of death. He could identify with that. His old culture had been replaced.

He handed the sheath back to the man and moved on.

Yet there was something buried in him. He hardly was aware of it—a momentary longing—nothing more than a stray hair he brushed from his forehead. But it left a feeling—a smothered loss that would open—if he let it.

He moved to the next counter. He felt the old land bridge, the old migration trail. But he decided to leave it unexplored, undiscovered. He had been raised a Christian. It was his heritage now. Everything he had came from it. Job, Daniel, Isaiah were his stories. Once he had been left out of God's kingdom—but through Christ, he could make a quantum leap and be transformed into a new being. It was Lutheran physics. He took a breath. It didn't sound so strange.

There were some antique crosses. He saw one his wife would like. He bought it and left the store. God was still paying attention, the way he saw it.

Later, when he picked up his wife at her sister's house, he heard his brothers-in-law talking about the record snow. He heard about their loss of jobs, their uncertainties. His wife talked more about her wobbly position. Her husband worked full time, but he had a one-year renewable contract at the University of Minnesota at Morris, which supplied little security. Even if he had tenure, the board of regents was trying to remove tenure. They were turning quarters into semesters. Who knew what would happen? He sat uncomfortably as his wife talked to her family about their situation. A new professor was taking his environment course next year. The new professor had already chosen books for it. He'd already given written preference for his classroom. And if the university hired someone else permanently, wouldn't it be a woman or a minority to fill the diversity requirement? But wasn't he a minority? Could he prove it? Was he enrolled? The new professor's perky new wife had come to a faculty party. He had heard her say that she wanted to teach also.

Who was his own wife to talk about his position as if she were part of it? She should be concerned with the insecurity of her own job and leave him alone. And what if the Manor turned out his father? she asked. What would they do then? And what were they going to do with her mother?

At least they didn't have children, one of her sisters said. He saw his wife's niece in the corner. The one who had stayed with them. The one who played the piano. He smiled at her. She seemed shy. She seemed older.

On the way back to Morris, he gave his wife the antique cross he bought.

"It'll be all right," he told her, and she reached her hand across the seat toward him.

In April, the snow in his yard began to thaw. On the news, there were worries about the melting of the heavy snows that had fallen that winter.

His father was holding up.

He stopped by Lake Osakis one evening on his way from the Manor.

He remembered even during the week, when the fishermen and vacationers were gone back to the cities, and it was quiet, the lake was still restless and speaking. But it was too early for lake traffic. The lake had not thawed. He could see the thin ice sheets in places.

He remembered the birds. The network of their calling. The family of the land, which included the water, the boats upon it, the waves behind them. The relationship of all. Overlapping. Changing. Conflicting. Connected.

They were defined by landscape. More than they knew. Maybe even history was shaped by the land.

He sighed as he read in his study that night. There was something artificial and tedious about it. Something in him bucked against it. Yet reading and teaching were his life.

When he fell behind in grade school, his parents had prayed for him. With ceremony, they had taken him to the Osakis library for a library card. It was a ticket to understanding. He was enrolled in the summer reading program at the library. The library card was Elisha's chariot. He remembered his father saying that. He remembered the discomfort he felt in school. His struggle to get through Concordia College. His parents were praying for him. He knew it. The God of their heaven would defend him from Sennacherib, who would keep him from getting through school. But once in a while as he sat in his study or his office at the Morris campus, he had to walk away from his rows of books.

The land was someone telling him a story. His Indian grandfather. Maybe his real father. No, his father wouldn't tell stories. No one who abandoned a woman and baby would hear the land. Maybe a great-grandfather or an ancestor. He didn't know. But he felt someone there. He didn't believe in ghosts. But there were voices that came up out of the land and spoke with the land's voices.

He thought of the shadow world. The fog from the melting snow. He saw it around the streetlights in front of his house because the temperature that evening was above freezing.

He heard the call of something beyond. It was in himself that he found his community. Wherever he had come from. Whatever his origin.

The parents who raised him. They were his source. He had to struggle through his own divided territory. He felt he had nothing definite, but was to be satisfied as if he did.

When he wrote a paper, it changed a hundred times. Even after he gave it at a conference, it changed. He would hear different sentences than he had presented, and he would go back and change them. He could collect his conference papers. Maybe the essays would be his book. Maybe he'd already written it.

He felt like a spur. An aftergrowth. Something out of place like the land in the civilized world before him. He would take what he had been given and make his own trail through it. Ceremony had been taken from him as the wilderness had been taken from the land.

He heard the bedroom radio and decided that his wife was in bed. But he stayed at the window. He thought of the new professor already moving on to a different school. It was not impossible. He had come suddenly. He could leave suddenly.

In May, the Red River, which flowed north because of the Continental Divide, was rising from the melting snow.

Friday after his classes, they drove through water-logged fields to his wife's sisters' and mother's places near Moorhead, but there was nothing he could do. He sandbagged with his wife's sisters and brothers-in-law in the cold until his arms ached and he sat with his wife in her sister's house.

He knew there was the threat of flood, but the sandbags on top of the dikes that lined the river would hold.

Her mother was confused when they talked to her about the rising river. They told her she couldn't stay at her house. She couldn't stay alone.

The cold moved into the river, the river moved into the trees, the trees into the fields. Cold water gushed across the roads. Highways were closed. When the dikes broke, the basements sucked the water into them. Grand Forks in North Dakota, to the north, went under.

Water stood in the fields. The surface of the flood froze. Cattle stepped onto the ice and fell through. They went into a hypothermic daze and sank into the water.

There was more floodwater than a mirror in a box could multiply. He felt the swirling energies of the water. The long stretch of quiet. The suck noises. The silence again.

The gravity pulled time into it also. The newspapers remembered other floods. The ministers remembered Noah. He thought of the longing and hunger of the land, like his, for peace and rest.

The flood was the furniture of nature. The flood moved into the houses.

"We make a mess of the land. It makes a mess of us. We fight ourselves when we subdue nature," he told his

"Literature and the Environment" class when he returned to Morris. "We find the same love, hunger, barbarism in the land as we find in ourselves."

God was hidden in the earth, the grass, herbs, trees, the hole in the ice-fishing house, the watery fish beneath it, the moon, the sun, the stars like fish moving through the heavens.

He tried out some of his ideas on the class and received puzzled looks.

His wife was on the phone with her family all the time. He thought of the phone bill she would have to pay.

It was because of the water from more of the melting snow.

Before he knew it, two of his wife's sisters and their families stayed with them for a night in Morris. There were gymnasiums and churches and VFW halls open for the flood victims from Grand Forks to Moorhead to Morris.

Actually, the sisters' houses hadn't flooded, but the Red River threatened. He discovered he didn't have a place to sleep. He didn't have a sleeping bag or a cot, but there was a couch in the student lounge in his building at the Morris campus. He went there, but found the door locked. He went to his office and slept in his coat on the floor for the night. He wore his gloves. He used the sweater from behind the door as a pillow. Once in the night he woke with an ache in his four-toed foot.

In the morning when he returned, his small house was full of cooking smells, bacon and eggs and coffee. His house was full of noise. The children were watching television with the volume up. The radio was on. The women's voices were heard over the men's. His wife had left for work. He was alone with them. He wanted them out of his house. They hardly knew he was there. They considered it their sister's house. He didn't matter to them. He just lived there as their sister's husband. He had no place to go but the university and the Manor.

How long would his father hold on? He only had strength to mumble now, passing in and out of consciousness. His father hardly recognized him anymore.

There was a call for help along the Red River. He went with two of his brothers-in-law to Grand Forks.

At first, the floodwater was quiet as they bagged sand for levees. Then he heard the noises. They were almost inaudible. The earth was moaning. Gulching. Mumbling. Something more like mumbling. The animals. The elements. Something he did not recognize. The sound of the land was always there.

He heard the diesel-powered pumps and generators, the tractors, the snowplows. The gas-powered generators that ran the sump pumps to suck water out of basements.

The water had happened so quickly that people were

stranded in their houses. His brothers-in-law were a part of the rescue crews. He went with them.

His wife didn't want him to go, but he felt he had to act. Hadn't his father lifted his mother's casket, gaining strength as he lifted?

The woman in Grand Forks was distraught. A grandmother, he supposed. She hadn't been able to find her son and his family, who should have come from their farm.

The men drove as far as they could, then got the boat out of the truck. They rowed against the current toward a farmhouse.

His brother-in-law called out, but no one was there. Where were the people? Had they tried to walk? There was another abandoned farmhouse down the road. The road was under water. The ice chunks broke the propeller on the small motor of the aluminum boat. The boat

was being swept sideways. He couldn't row like his brothers-in-law. He hit the ice with his oar and broke some of it. One of his brothers-in-law helped him row. The aluminum boat made slow progress.

"Let's give up," one of his brothers-in-law said.

"—go back," the other one started his sentence at the end.

"We can't give up," he told his brothers-in-law.

"What makes you think the people made it to the next house?"

He saw the farmhouse was at least a half-mile ahead

and the water was rising. They could turn back. They could not be blamed.

He agreed they were foolish to go on. They were asking for trouble. But something moved in him. He told his two brothers-in-law they had to try.

"Maybe the family is there—"

He listened to his brothers-in-law grumble. But he heard the voice of the land. *Conditions could change changing conditions.* The message from the land was to him. The land could change men by its challenges. He could be more or less than he thought, because of his interaction with the land.

"We have to try one more farmhouse—"

The brothers-in-law listened to what he said. They decided to keep going. He wanted to meet the challenge of the flood. But the boat was snagged on the ice. No amount of pounding with the oar would break it. He got out of the boat and crawled on his belly to the abandoned farmhouse.

One of his brothers-in-law called him back to the boat. "If the ice breaks, you'd be in several feet of frigid water. If the water keeps rising, it will cover the ice."

His brothers-in-law would probably not be able to save him.

But he kept going. He made it to the house. He stepped through an open window. Passed through the house once. Twice. He shouted. No one answered. He went upstairs. He went back downstairs. There in the kitchen, on a counter, was a couple with a child curled up between them. They were dazed, the child unconscious. He tried to rouse the man. He shook his shoulder until the man stirred. They were nearly frozen to death. They were disoriented. "Get up." He pulled the man. The man motioned he wanted to get their wet clothes. "No," he said. He told the man to stay with the child. He lifted the nearly naked woman from the counter and carried her to the door. He stepped onto the ice, which was now covered with a thin layer of water.

The cold water hurt his feet as if it were the hot water spilling from under the dashboard of his car. There was no difference in the pain of hot and cold. He was perceiving himself in a new light. He was aware of his surroundings more than he'd ever been. He was responsible. He felt the land rush into his head with a jagged realization. It could both hurt and help. He felt the determination rush into his head. He was doing what his father would have done. His mother. He had been inaudible in his parents' house. He was inaudible in the landscape. Now he felt he was heard.

One of his brothers-in-law stepped over the ice in the rising water. The brother-in-law told the woman to crawl toward him, but she couldn't respond. He pushed her over the ice. His brother-in-law pulled her to the boat. He saw the bluish white skin of the woman who wore only underpants and a bra. He saw the goose-bumped and prickled skin around the upper part of her thighs. He tried not to look at her crevices, her wet bra clinging to her breasts, the hair in places his wife didn't have hair. When she was in the boat, he crawled back for the man and the child.

His teeth chattered. He felt he had fish in his mouth. There were alternatives. Things didn't have to go the way it seemed they would. This was one of those times. He would act on it. He wouldn't retreat. He would go ahead.

He slipped on the porch as he went back into the house. He was numb and hardly felt the knock of the floor on his head.

He was so cold, it was hard to move. The water was coming into the house. He thought he heard his niece's music in the water that pushed past the farmhouse. He thought he heard her notes in the water that spilled across the floor. What if the water lifted the house off its foundation? What if he floated away in it? He had to get the child. He tried to get up. His legs were stiff. For a moment, he couldn't find the air to stand up in. Then his legs straightened and he was making his way to the kitchen. He lifted the child from the counter and went to the door. The child looked asleep, or dead. But he saw a faint pulse in its neck. A brother-in-law was waiting at the door to carry the child to the boat.

He returned for the man. His niece's concert was louder now.

Which one of his brothers-in-law was the niece's father? Neither one deserved her.

The man was heavy and he couldn't lift him from the counter. The man tried to move, but couldn't. His arms and legs were hard. He tried to call for his brothers-in-law but by now, they probably had to hold the boat steady and couldn't help. He tried again to lift the man and when he couldn't, he pulled him to the floor with a jerk. The man's body splashed in the layer of cold water in the kitchen. He tried to pull him across the floor, slipping several times. The man groaned, and seemed to be trying to help, but he couldn't move his arms and legs.

He went to the front door.

"Bring a rope. I can't lift him."

The brothers-in-law called him back to the boat. He saw how low the boat sat in the water. How could it hold two more men?

"Throw that rope," he insisted.

He saw the boat twist in the water that swirled around it. He saw his brothers-in-law row to hold it steady.

He crawled toward the boat on the ice. A brother-in-law threw a rope. He took it and threw one end back.

"Tie it to the bow."

"We got to get this child out of the cold."

He saw his brothers-in-law without their coats. The one shivered so hard he could hardly talk.

He crawled back to the house with the loose end of the rope. He tied it around the man's foot but it came undone. He tried to push him across the floor when he saw the rope pull from the kitchen. He couldn't reach it. He couldn't give up. He couldn't leave the man. There was salvation in the world. He'd heard it all his life. His strength was in his weakness. Jesus, he called.

Suddenly a brother-in-law was there with the rope. He helped him tie it around the man's chest.

"The boat is pulling away from the house," the brother-in-law said. "It will help move him—"

They tried to lift him, but couldn't. Then they pushed the man when they felt the tug of the rope. Slowly they got him across the floor and out the door. They sledded him over the ice toward the boat, skinning his arms and back and legs.

In the boat, they covered the people with their coats. Why hadn't they brought blankets? How long would it be until they got back to the road, and into the rescue vehicle on the way to the hospital behind the snowplow?

The Red River flowed north. Now they rowed with the current back to Grand Forks. The boat was overloaded. The three people were near death, he thought, the three of them who rescued the family were suffering from hypothermia.

"Row! Row!" he shouted at his brothers-in-law, not looking at the people rigid in the boat, but at the cold, sunny sky. He heard his father at the Manor. "Row," he said. He heard his ancestors, whoever they were, who had migrated across the land. He heard the buffalo.

"Row," they snorted. He heard the land. "Row!" it said as the water carried them with its voice. Its tune.

The man who heard the land saw his own name in the newspaper. The story of the rescue that he and his brothers-in-law made was in the front section. There was a picture of the couple recovering in the hospital. Their child wrapped in a blanket between them. How had they survived? How had they come back to life?

It was his relationship to the land that enabled him to became a man. That's what the land said.

For once, he didn't hear the wind of his own concerns, his inconsiderateness of the earth, of the animals, of everything else.

He had been kicked into this life in a parsonage between parents who whitewashed the world for him. Dehorned it. Dethorned it. Now his father was caught on the horns he had erased for him.

At least he wasn't bringing anyone else into life, but that wasn't the point. It wasn't solved by that. In fact, it was an indication of his not taking part. It was a shrinking back. A cowardliness.

The new professor did not go away. He heard the new professor talking in the hall as he sat in his office reading an article in *National Geographic*. He was irritated anyway because it was a magazine his mother had not allowed him to read.

What could he have done if his parents hadn't held him back? No, his parents had not held him back. It was because of them he was reading the article.

The new professor was talking to a group of students. There were no students in his office at the moment. He thought he was open to students, but maybe they didn't stop by his office to talk as often as he thought. In fact, on his student evaluations, he sometimes read the comment that he was inaccessible. But his door was open. He was holding his office hours. Anyone could enter, he thought as he frowned.

Some of his colleagues had mentioned seeing his name in the newspaper. They had asked questions, but soon the event seemed to be forgotten.

He should be at the Manor, but instead he was reading that scientists estimated there had been some 15 billion years since the big bang. He read about the formation of quarks and antiquarks, the smallest constituents of matter. He read how they annihilated one another, but fortunately, there were more quarks than antiquarks. It was the unevenness of the universe that clumped galaxies together. It seemed so vast it hurt his head.

He closed his office door so he could concentrate. He thought he should go to the Manor, but his father was not aware he was there any longer.

He sat alone in his office. He read about the universe

moving toward some mysterious gravitational source whose location remained unknown. He read about dark matter and black holes. The universe frightened him as he read. He remembered when he thought his own galaxy was the entire universe. But the Milky Way with its billions of stars was only part of a galaxy, which was a part of other galaxies, which were parts of others, all moving outward toward some destination.

Then he read about the quasars, some 14 billion light years away. They might be a stage young galaxies go through. But despite the vast numbers of stars, the universe was still mainly emptiness. Cold and sometimes flickering with explosive energy.

He shut the *National Geographic* when he heard a burst of laughter from the new professor and the students in the hall.

He left his office and the building and got in his car and drove to his barbershop.

The voice of the land was in his head. He had heard it, not with his ears, but with his understanding and recognition. They had been joined. His body was of the earth. But the earth was also something else. A redefinition of time and space from which it came. And how did the land relate to space?

When he returned to his office, he wrote: MASS AND ENERGY AND TIME AND SPACE.

In his head the past moved. He felt the unknown. He felt the longing of time and the land when God was the flood of being. He felt biblical. That was his heritage. Well, he'd take it then. Use it in his own way. Make God sorry he'd ripped him out of his heritage. Detribalized him.

But what was his heritage? Wasn't it the Bible stories he'd heard all his life? *If he ran with the footmen and they wearied him, how could he contend with the horses?* Jeremiah 12:5. He knew the footmen of his own discouragement. He knew the horses also.

He wasn't heard in department meetings, just as the trees and hills and the sky weren't heard. No one realized they were separate parts. They were not just nature, they were himself. The bird's song he could hear in his own yard was part of himself calling in an unlearned language, a forgotten language probably, with an unknown message; a stranger to his stranger. A language of words that had to go together in a different way.

When he turned into his drive that evening, he saw the fir tree beside the house. Near the woodpile, the thick branches moved slightly, shifting as if underwater. The branches were part of the trunk, yet they moved independently. Separately. They were parts of himself not recognized, ignored, left among those things of which he was unaware by choice. How many things could he notice? The branches nodding separately like heads, some saying yes, some no.

They were probably mostly glad they no longer carried the weight of snow.

Sometimes he felt he would know something, when the variables clicked.

The wild bosom of Abraham left a chair on a bridge across the Red River when the flood receded. He saw the photo in the Morris newspaper. He showed it to his father when he visited the Manor. But his father didn't respond. He seemed to grow weaker each visit.

He also was a depressed field, he thought as he drove back to Morris for a department meeting where everyone would be buzzing about the promotion of the new professor. He imagined the water that filled his life. It swirled in his basement floating boxes to the ceiling, opening cabinets, displacing everything, turning over the tables and chairs. Then the muck afterwards. The furniture of nature was the trees, the topsoil, the river that flooded a bridge, leaving a chair in the highest limbs in case anyone wanted to sit there.

He felt the flood had been much like the words in the book he should write.

He thought of the flood as an invasion of Sennacherib.

Sometimes he thought he could hear the metal deer from Germany.

In the department meeting, he thought of the story of the bird and the bright ball the fisherman kept in a box. The bird was his birth mother who became another mother to release him from the box and return him to the sky where he belonged.

He liked the way the story turned to whatever light

was needed. The way he saw Bible stories becoming whatever shape was needed.

He waited after the department meeting.

He asked again to teach his "Literature and the Environment" course, and not be bypassed by the new professor who was taking his courses. Taking his trips. Who could sit in the department meetings and say something significant.

"How are your book, your published articles?" the head of the department asked.

"They aren't," he answered.

Why didn't the department head ask how his father was? How many trips he had made to the Manor since the school year began? How many classes he had taught? How many papers he had graded? How many bags had he stuffed with sand? Didn't the department head remember his name in the newspaper?

From his window, he heard the squall of a bird or a squirrel.

Yes, the new professor would teach his environment course. Maybe he would teach "Literature and Religion." "Literature and History." He had to invent a new course.

There was a party for English majors at the department head's house. He hated parties. He and his wife huddled together trying to find a presence they did not have as individuals.

The new professor and his wife had just returned

from a weekend camping trip. They moved easily around the room talking to students and colleagues. But when he introduced his wife to the students, they tried to think of something to say, and when he said something, he wished he had said nothing. The students looked around for someone else to talk to.

"Do you camp?" the new professor asked, coming upon them in his round of people.

"No," his wife said. They didn't. There was the silence again. Why did she have to answer? Why didn't she leave the conversation to him?

"We plan to—next summer," he said.

"You don't need a summer. You can go to the Boundary Waters in a weekend."

"Well, you have Tuesday and Thursday classes, so you can have long weekends."

The wife of the new professor smiled at her husband as though it were something he should be proud of.

His wife looked at him. His classes were spread through the week, from Monday mornings to Friday afternoons.

"Someone has to hold the fort," he said.

He thought how his classrooms were a landscape. He saw his students as trees and shrubs, deer and fish. He thought how he went camping with his students in class discussions.

He and his wife didn't particularly like to be outside. She planted a few flowers. Tended her roses. He shoveled snow and mowed the yard. Why would he hear the land? Wasn't the land to him more of an idea?

Another afternoon, when he returned to Morris from the Manor, he wrote: THE LAND WAS ONE BEFORE IT BROKE INTO CONTINENTS.

The book he was writing flooded with thoughts that didn't go together. Sometimes he thought he heard the land say, *the man who heard the land heard questions.* But the land had a message for him. It was a transmitter of something beyond itself. If only he could be a receptor of that message.

He knew nature let itself be used. It lived as men's dreams lived. In the day world, dreams seemed not to exist. They could be forgotten. Overlooked. It could seem as if they didn't exist. But go for a night without dreams, or several nights, and he would be separated from his mooring, his reason, his rational perception and behavior. Things were not as straight as he saw them. The knowledge he had built through observations and research could be toppled. Was there one truth? Were there several truths? Were there subtruths that played a part? Were there millions of years of history on earth? Was there another history before his father's six-thousand-year history since Adam? Were there several creations of the world? Was it possible to know? He wanted to think. Had dinosaurs walked with an earlier version of man?

Was it all reconcilable? Or was there only the small fort of civilization, beyond which was the unknown? He watched the fir tree move like water on Lake Osakis.

Sennacherib meant *not the first born*. Maybe this wasn't the first world. How could dinosaurs and millions of years of history fit into the six thousand years since Adam? There had to be some explanation.

He would invent time that was shorter than it seemed. Like the fish trap he tried to invent as a boy, which wouldn't hook the fish by their mouths.

He had taught the importance of the land and animals in his "Literature and the Environment" course, yet a raccoon got under the small deck in back of his house and scratched at his basement window in the window well. He decided to call animal control service. Before they came, he stood looking at the raccoon. It seemed to want in.

Late the following afternoon, a green truck came. The man set a live trap in his backyard, then left.

The next morning, he saw the cage with the raccoon in it.

He was at the kitchen table when the man came to pick it up. The man seemed to say something to the raccoon as he walked through the yard with it, but when he got to the truck, he slammed the cage into the city truck. The racket of the metal cage hitting the truck startled him in the house. What must it have sounded like to the raccoon and to other animals in other traps in the enclosed truck? The raccoon was trapped because it was hungry.

He went outside when the truck left. He saw the ground where the cage had been. The raccoon had clawed at the cage through the night until it had clawed up all the grass. Though there was no hope of release, it didn't give up.

He thought how the raccoon had struggled against hopelessness. Maybe he was trapped. Maybe someday his books and articles would be published. His courses would be his own. Maybe he would write several articles about time and the land. Then a book.

The animal control service left an empty cage in his backyard for several days. Raccoons usually were in pairs, his wife said when she came home from work. What happened to the mate? That's why the cage was there.

She handed him a package from her bag. She had framed the newspaper article of the flood, the picture of the family they rescued, and a picture of him and his brothers-in-law that hadn't made the paper.

"Where did you get this?"

"You told me the paper had taken more pictures. I called them and got the one of you."

In June, there were further complications in his father's health. One organ responded to another. He had spent another weekend at the Manor beside his bed.

When he returned to his house Sunday evening, he found his wife crying in the kitchen. She was in the semi-dark and he didn't see her at first. He knew she didn't want to be seen, but he came into the kitchen before she heard him. He had left his car in the drive in case he had to return to the Manor.

"What's the matter?" he asked.

It was her job. She found the stress intolerable. She couldn't go back.

He said he would help her write a letter of resignation. She had years of experience. She would find another job.

He stood a moment by her chair, then knelt before her.

"There are a lot of people looking for work," she said. "I've seen some of their applications. My boss asked what I thought about their qualifications. It isn't easy to find another job."

He reached for her and held her in his arms. He felt awkward. She responded awkwardly. But there was a small spark in the darkness of their universe.

He was reading a magazine article about the Germans making Indian camps for summer retreats—but it was the nineteenth-century Plains Indian they copied. Something that had disappeared. How he longed for it too.

He heard the phone. He heard his wife calling him. It was the Manor about his father.

He would have to go.

His father's funeral was on a cold, early summer day.

And it came to pass that the beggar died, and was carried by the angels into Abraham's bosom; the rich man died also, and was buried;

And in hell he lifted up his eyes, being in torment, and saw Abraham far off, and Lazarus in his bosom. Luke 16:22–23

He stood over his father's grave in the raw cemetery. He wanted to ask, *why did you have Sennacherib on the wall?*

He wanted to say, *there probably were mysteries buried in the land.* They would be discovered from time to time. But the important lesson was the work and dignity and endurance it took to live.

He stood with his wife at his father's grave. He heard the sound of the land, turning on its trip around the sun, feeling phased out, cut back, stepped on. He was part of the earth. Even with the odds against him, he would endure. Maybe his father would have said the earth was being stripped, beaten as Christ had been before crucifixion. The pattern the land only followed.

He watched a cardinal build her nest in the bush outside his window. Later, he saw the babies with their beaks open. It was their instinct to open their mouths and call for heaven to pick them up. But their parents put food in their mouths while they were calling, giving them what they didn't want. Yet they continued to call.

The bird belonged to the sky and earth. He could transport the moon from its imprisonment in a box by one shape becoming another. He was that shape-changer. His thoughts could free him with different kinds of thinking.

126   The man who heard the land heard NOW.

When he heard the land he was not concerned with getting to the next point in time. But with being more into the now.

When they would talk in class, his Indian students spoke about the importance of words, of stories. They were concerned with memory, where the stories were carried. They were concerned with the loss of their language.

Maybe he would write about the disruption of land as a disruption of language. Or was it the other way?

Did language know emissions, colonization, global warming, burning of fossil fuels, escalating changes? Were there denials of the deterioration of its world? The sickness at the heart? Was its core crying out?

The new professor came from a line of teachers, while he came from nowhere. He had been left on the steps of a minister and his wife who would dim the world of possibilities for him. He carried his parents' narrow life of poverty and inflexibility. Yet he also understood how everything was reciprocal as he read the papers of his Indian students. Everything belonged to a pattern. The cradle-board headpiece symbolized the rainbow. The blanket was the clouds. The rawhide string zigzagged across the blanket like lightning or the forces of the wind. There was something about the powers of the universe or the holy people. It sounded far away and out of bounds for him. But that was his mother rumbling around in his head as though she looked for a utensil in a kitchen drawer. He remembered sometimes he had heard her in the morning when he woke.

He sat in his chair in his office in the quiet building and dozed as he thought. But a door closed somewhere, and he woke. Time was spiral, he thought. An orbiting line that could result in spaces both small and large. Syncretic. What did that word mean in the context of his thought?

The simultaneity of time. Should he write that down? The light / the dark / the grass that came before the sun, which made it grow. The small before the large? The second before the first? Could that be right? He turned to Genesis. The first day, God divided the light from dark. The second day, he made the heavens. The third, the sea and the earth with the trees and grasses on it. The forth the sun, moon, and stars. What did that mean? There was light before the sun? Grass could grow in that light? There was a time before the earth rotated, before the sun for the day and night? There's a mystery there.

The sun was not created until the fourth day. But there was light from the first pages of the Bible. But it didn't take a sun to make light. Well, it did, but there could be light independent of the sun. Energy was light. The big bang was light. Anger, also, was light.

He wondered about the possibility of a time embedded in a time, as the center of the spiral was embedded in the outer. No, he thought as he sat in his office and returned to reading his students' papers. He would let it go.

He liked the smell of lilacs in the neighbor's yard. Through the window of his study that night, he saw the white lilac bush of the moon. He could almost smell it in the sky.

In the newspaper, a satellite photo of a hurricane in the Caribbean looked like the hole in a funnel web he'd seen in the corner of the basement window.

He put the newspaper aside and continued reading his students' papers so he could turn in their grades for the spring quarter they had just finished.

He was on a journey to a destination. Heaven, his father had preached. But he also was on a journey to the *Now*. He was on several journeys to separate places. Irreconcilable.

The *Now* frightened him. He was accountable. On the other journey, he was not as responsible. He was moving toward a point where he wasn't as yet. He was always going, but not arrived. But in the *Now*, he could arrive.

He was trying to find a sense of place in his placelessness. The land was not his home. That was his father speaking. But the land said he belonged to it also. Could he be both? As body and mind were separate yet cohabitated?

His niece who played the piano was in trouble. His wife told him as they ate at Don's Restaurant on Saturday night. How could that be?

"She's pregnant," his wife said. "Nearly seven months."

He couldn't believe what he was hearing. "Was she raped?" he asked, forgetting the walleye he was about to eat. He had seen her since she was pregnant, yet had not known.

"No. It was some boy she dated," his wife told him. "She hid it as long as she could."

He didn't even know she was dating. "Will she get married?" he asked.

"I don't think so."

"What will she do?"

"My sister said she'd keep it," his wife said, and reminded him of his dinner.

His niece had played the land for him on her piano, now she would—what was he thinking?—flood.

The man who heard the land also heard his wife.

She had quit her job and was looking for another one. But jobs were hard to find.

She had figured how long they could go without her working. They would use their savings for mortgage payments when the time came. They could buy food and pay bills with his salary from the university. But what if he lost his job? he asked. She had figured that too. She knew how long it would be until they couldn't make mortgage payments and would have to move in with one of her sisters. Or her mother. Someone would have to take care of her mother eventually.

Was that how the land felt? What if he faced extinction like some of the species? Like Indian tribes? Except they survived. Some of them anyway.

He sat at the table looking at his wife as they ate breakfast. He had just finished taking care of his parents. Now someone else was in line?

"We don't have to stay in Morris," his wife said.

"I still work at the university," he told her. "I couldn't live with your sisters," he said. "Maybe your mother. But we won't have to do that."

"If we lived closer to Moorhead, we could help my niece—"

He looked at his wife as he buttered his toast.

"I think they'll be looking for help," she said. "I know my sister will soon be complaining about the pregnancy."

"We can help and still live in Morris."

"We could live in my mother's house with my mother, the niece, and the baby. You could commute to Morris."

"I don't want to commute. I want to be in my house as long as I teach at Morris."

"I could clear out my workroom—"

"I don't want your niece and her baby to live with us."

"I could go to Moorhead when they needed me—"

"I don't want you to be away from Morris."

Now it was his wife who looked at him.

On Saturday, he drove to the Osakis cemetery to see how his father's grave had been closed. He knew it was too soon for the date to be etched on the stone. He stood over the graves of both his parents.

He knew there was a summer storm on the horizon. He stood in the cemetery as long as he could, then ran to the car when the wind hit and the first drops fell. He tried to find a weather report on the radio, but got static. He changed the station and found nothing. The sky was a glass-plate window. The light flashed across it. Glared in his eyes.

There were great dark clouds across the sky. But there was a hole where the sun still shone through. He felt the thunder zigzagging across the clouds. Something was holding him in place.

He drove from the cemetery, quickly, back toward Morris. He remembered the times he and his father had been together. He could see his father's car like a toy crossing the flat Minnesota landscape toward the parsonage in Osakis, the windshield wipers flapping like some giant insect's wings. Now he thought of his own car drifting across the land. Somewhere in the wind, he heard the land. At one time, he knew the land said *the man who heard the land heard himself.* But now it seemed to say he also heard something other than himself. Was the message of the land changing? Was it like a conversation? Was it contradictory?

When he looked at the land, he thought a tiny particle had exploded. It still sounded in the radio static. *Because of God,* he heard his father's voice. Variability and relativity and the changes of heat on mass had caused the land where he drove.

He liked to let his thoughts flood over the road with

the storm. He himself followed a pattern of the universe because he was made from it. There was interchange between them, he liked to think. The force of rebirth infused his spirit. Was that his father again? He wished he could understand the concept of reconciliation, or at least make use of it somehow.

For him, above the storm clouds, the vast constellations of his thoughts were shaped like Gumby and Pokey. The stars were cacti on the floor of the universe. The open range. The loneliness that caused the big bang. He thought of his niece. Was the bang not like the explosion of a man into a woman, the connecting of one to the other, cells combining, dividing, an eternal being brought forth? Sucked inward or outward in an upward-moving never-ending life. Transforming like the bird who became a child who wanted a bright ball in a box. He wanted his universe full of mothballs rising and sinking. The magic of his boy's imagination. The great mystery of the universe was as simple as transformation. A story that had different meanings and endings as diffuse as those who heard and told them.

133

He would never know who he was. Something that was his had been taken. Or if he knew who he was, he would never know where he came from. A door had been closed. Whole landscapes outside of himself were off-limits.

He thought how everything went away. He was content to let it go. He was a man whose thought-life was the landscape in which he lived. Maybe the earth would shove and push until he broke open and gave something of himself.

After supper one evening, he mowed the lawn. Afterwards he sat on the deck. His wife came to the door. He asked if she wanted to go for a ride. She agreed.

He drove down a county road near Morris and stopped. They walked farther that evening than they had walked in a long time. It was close to dark before they turned back toward the car.

How often the land was *hidden under*, he thought as he walked beside his wife. Suddenly he realized there were three deer beside the road. Hadn't they heard him coming? They didn't run, but they were watching. He didn't run, but walked past them watching from the corner of his eye. He took his wife's hand, telling her without words not to be frightened, to be quiet as she walked. She knew they were there too. He held her hand firmly. What a moment. He was a man standing in the corner of his eye, while the larger man walked with his wife past the deer beside the road. He felt the immensity of them.

If he had a rifle, he could shoot one and bring it out of its wildness. The deer belonged to a world that moved at night. Wild and natural as dreams. He could walk near, recognize the otherness of that world, even be a distant part of it, but he could not completely enter. They were beyond a boundary he could not cross. He was not the whole world. His father had not hidden that information from him. His father had not known how to tell him. Maybe his father had never felt what he was feeling now.

"Can you imagine anyone shooting them?" his wife asked when they were past the deer, and then he couldn't.

"But the hunters say there are so many of them, they would starve in the winter anyway," he told his wife.

On the dark road, the stars were brighter than they were in Morris. But the sky was still full of dullness. What must the stars have looked like on clear nights long ago? They must have snapped like electricity. The moon lighting them, shining through the hide of the teepee. It made him feel sick. Yet he couldn't stand looking back. He had to go ahead.

The deer woke him from sleep that night. Or the thought of the deer woke him. He got up without waking his wife and opened the back door. He stood on his deck. He was on fire with darkness. He stood under the night-light of the moon. The moon was the sun on the dark night in his yard. He closed his eyes. He felt the deer nibbling somewhere in the woods along the road where he had walked with his wife. He longed for them. They had seen in him a man who was passing. Maybe they had sensed he was not a threat. He felt one with the earth and the dull light of the moon. He let out his breath from his body, but did not see it in the night air that was chilly though it was summer.

He remembered the raccoon that had been under the deck. He had heard its language. It had lost its mate somehow. Everything came in pairs. He remembered reading that in one of the science journals. The raccoon was voicing its loneliness. He sat on the deck with his head in his hands. He felt the deathly loneliness of the land that God must have felt too, and had cried out for the other—for an earth full of people who would cause him more distress that he had ever known. Why did he do it? For love. He would risk even his own son. Hadn't that been his father's message all his life? Was he just now understanding?

It was worth the trouble. He felt God's hand reach down and take his. The deer knew it. The raccoon. The cardinals.

He looked up through the darkness. He wanted to see the deer in his yard. The raccoon. The cardinals asleep somewhere in the trees. The deer also were part of his family he lost. They were not different from him.

He felt the enormity of existence swallow him, and in that vastness, he felt the others. He thought of long ago. He thought of Israel as they crossed into the promised land, which they knew was inhabited by tribes stronger than they were. He thought of his wife and others without jobs who were in a place with problems larger than they were. Everything in its time and space was bombarded by significance.

He read the job list in the *Chronicle of Higher Education*. He already knew how grim the market was. He heard it at conferences. He knew it from others. Besides, he had a job. The university always would need someone to teach what others didn't want to teach. To teach the summer sessions no one wanted. To ease into semesters from which others would retire.

Besides, his wife was a good accountant. She would find a job.

He sat in his office at the Morris campus before the summer session began. There had been a few days he and his wife could have gone somewhere, but she was looking for work, even part-time work. If they went someplace, it would have been to one of her sisters'. Probably the one with the pregnant niece.

He remembered his father in the field. *The man who heard the land heard Genesis.* He remembered his father working in his field. *In the sweat of your face you will eat bread, for out of the dust you were taken.*

It got back to the land. The land was his work. He heard its unanswerable questions, its mysteries. Its conflicts. He heard the force of its ties. Its implications. Its patterns and relationships. When he heard the land, he knew he was hearing the underlying principles that bound his life. They were there, almost inaudible. Something like a heartbeat.

He could stand in front of a classroom and open it for the students. In his first awkwardness, they felt their awkwardness. He recovered from his silence. They recovered from theirs.

Abraham's bosom was the Scriptures, the exchange of breath, the meaning, he said in his "Writings on Faith" course. Their discussions and essays would be a portage to an understanding, the way Vikings and later the French voyageurs carried their boats and canoes and baggage overland between waters.

They were made from the land and the stars. Their words connected like birds' nests across the yards— with a string of air between them, but threaded together nonetheless.

It was the Bible that opened up possibilities. The anthology of different voices through time. The Bible gave his world an expanding relativity. Yet when he pushed

toward the outer walls, there was something holding firm. He could be an outsider in the world, but with faith he could make it work. Could belief be his ceremony?

Could faith find his wife a full-time job, and not the temporary office work she hated? he thought as he watched her knit a sweater for the niece's baby.

Could faith find his niece a husband? he thought as he saw her during an awkward visit they finally made.

Could faith write a book? he thought on the way back to Morris. Find a closeness to his wife? Give him classes he wanted to teach?

Even the stars in their courses fought against Sisera.
Judges 5:20. They would also fight against Sennacherib.
It seemed sometimes the universe was a toybox full
of space that could change. That could overlap. In quantum physics, light could act as both a particle and a wave.
Electrons could be both also. Maybe the way Christ was
human and divine at the same time.

He felt freed by what he couldn't understand. Its mystery pulled him forward. He had been snipped from one
place, grafted to another. But there was a long, long past
that would not let him go. He was a nomad who had to
stay in one place, boxed in a house, and in a drab, utilitarian office with metal furniture he shared with other
adjunct faculty. He was from a heritage that had once
known something different. Did he have brothers and
sisters? he thought as he sat in his office after class. Half
brothers and sisters?

Maybe his niece had eaten a berry and would give
birth to a bird who would restore the moon to the sky.
No, in that story, he was the one who would lose the
bright ball of light he kept in a box. Or he could look at
it in another way—the bird would take his bright ball of
isolation he kept in a box and return it to the sky.

The head of the department's term as head had been up
when spring quarter was over. He was going to step
down and teach full time in the fall. The new professor

decided he would become the head. No one challenged him. At least he would give up the "Literature and the Environment" course. It would be taught by the adjunct who developed it. It would be his again, he thought.

He sat in the department meeting and thought that he could be the department head, but no one would think of him. He would have to be permanent, tenured faculty to be department head. He was full time, but a full-time adjunct. Teaching all those courses at least gave him medical benefits. Others didn't have that, if they taught fewer than six courses. He needed benefits. Just think if he didn't have insurance when he lost his toe, his wife said.

When he said something about the department meeting, the new professor, who was the new head, said that actually Morris didn't have departments, but *disciplines*, and he would like the department meeting to be called the *discipline meeting*, and instead of department head, he was the *discipline coordinator*.

Actually, the smallest academic administrative units were the divisions, the old head of the department told him. English was in the Division of Humanities, which included seven other disciplines. Maybe he should be *head of division*.

The niece had the baby by the time they got to the hospital in Moorhead. The baby was in a little box on wheels, a bassinet, he guessed it was called. It wore a pink cap. The niece was in bed beside the baby. She could only stay in the hospital a day because of their health insurance. "Health Partners. Yes, the doctors and administrators are the partners. Not the patient," the brother-in-law said.

Tomorrow they would take her home.

He saw the niece sink in the bed, overwhelmed by the thought of taking care of a baby and living with her parents.

He stood in the hall talking to his brother-in-law. The rescue during the spring flood of the Red River had to be mentioned whenever they were together.

On the way to Morris, he was the first to speak. "Maybe we could take them. Maybe we could care for the baby in shifts. I can read and grade papers at home rather than the office. You're on part time. Maybe the niece could go to school a few afternoons a week. At Morris. She could study music. Do you think?"

His wife didn't respond to his question. "We don't mean anything to the doctors. It's a business. Look at those factory farms," his wife said.

"Your sister is not going to be kind to her," he said.

Was that how it was? He saw a baby he had no intention of taking care of, but he saw it, and wanted to care for it. Had it been that way for his parents when they'd seen him?

He opened the book he bought in Finland. It was full of hardship. Is that why he kept returning to it? Sometimes he just read a few lines here and there.

When I was born I had a herd of reindeer
five thousand odd
this summer they have all dropped dead
taken by God.

So now I've come to Obsorsk with the children,
made a fresh start,
hired myself to a Russian
though I'm ready to fall apart.

Did he really want his niece and her baby to live with them? He and his wife wouldn't be able to go out and eat all the time. Wouldn't the niece and baby interfere with his work? With his book that he wasn't writing? He might as well give them a place to live. Give her a chance to go to school.

His father had said that wisdom was the knowledge of God. But who was this God who had his kingdom in disarrangement, full of black holes and energy so dense nothing could move?

Late in the summer, the niece and baby moved into their house when the baby was several weeks old. The niece seemed relieved to be with them.

"She's more like us," he told his wife.

They listened to the baby cry the first night. He held his wife beside him as they listened. His wife smiled.

His niece was quiet when he drove her to the university to enroll for the fall. She was still large from carrying the baby. She was depressed. Getting her into classes would help, he thought.

She would ride with him two days a week while his wife took care of the baby. Sometimes he saw his wife's hands shake. He began holding the baby. He was nervous too. The baby was a bundle in his arms. A quark, he thought. It squirmed and put its fist to its mouth. It fretted and he didn't know what to do. His wife brought him the pacifier. He put it in the baby's mouth. It was quiet for a while, but soon fretted again. He went into the kitchen and warmed the bottle. Its eyes watched him as he fed it. It was a her. He couldn't call her *it*. He changed her diaper and put her in the crib. Soon it was asleep. She was asleep. Then he sat in the living room because he'd given up his study. If his niece and baby stayed, maybe next summer they could build a room onto the house.

Somewhere in the sky, he heard geese.

There was an environmental conference in Chicago, the new department head, the *discipline coordinator,* said as the fall term neared. Did he want to go?

No, he didn't, he answered, not even if the university paid for all of it, which they wouldn't.

The baby had become an Abraham's bosom for him. On Sundays, he went to the Lutheran church from time to time with his wife and niece and baby. He listened to the sermons. It was a ceremony he would choose. An act of faith. It was a decision, like marriage, like teaching. He would be a staple in the lives of his family.

The earth spoke mathematics. That's why he couldn't always understand it. It spoke the sound of principles or equations that had no words. It spoke pure thought. It was music, he thought, listening to the organ in church. Music had the sound that mathematics lacked.

How could he collect the land into a book? Would he
let someone else do it? That's what his history was. A supplanting by another. Not someone taking his classes, but a Christ's life that had overtaken his own life. It was the meaning of assimilation. Spiritual assimilation. Something had to take over the emptiness inside a man. Why not the Christian faith? Were those his father's words he was hearing? No, he was thinking his father's thoughts, but now they were innate.

A physics professor visited the Morris campus. The professor's talk was called "Earliest Moments in Creation." He drove to campus to hear the lecture. He saw the visiting professor come with a group of other professors from the chancellor's house, where they'd had dinner, he guessed. What would it be like to eat with the chancellor of the Morris campus? What did the house look like inside?

He took notes on the lecture.

The outward movement of the old explosion.

Cosmic inflation.

Quantum fluctuations.

The universe not absolutely uniformly distributed.

Gravity pulls matter together.

Sometimes he was lost in the lecture and slides and forgot to take notes or tie together his phrases.

How did structure form?

Most of the matter is not stars but dark matter, which is gravity.

Cold dark matter left over from the bang.

What would it be like to understand physics?

Yes, that's what he felt in the lecture.

He was raking leaves to the curb, probably the last time before the snow, when a man stopped in front of the house. Who was it? The man got out. He was a boy, really.

He was looking for his niece. What did the young man want?

"She's at school," he said.

"School?"

"She takes a class at the university."

He seemed to remember. "You're her uncle?"

"Yes."

Could he be the baby's father? Except for the first time he had heard she was pregnant, he had not thought who the father was. The young man stood by the car with his hands in the pockets of his jacket.

"She isn't here. Maybe when she gets back." Why didn't he know what to say? Of course she would be here when she got back. He always was saying the wrong thing.

"When will that be?"

"It depends."

Actually, he knew exactly when she would be back. His wife would pick her up when she got off work. In the meantime, the niece was practicing the piano at school.

He could call the music room and see if she wanted him to come there. It would lead the young man away from the baby.

"I'm raking the lawn. You can wait in your car."

"Is the baby in the house?"

"I put her down to sleep."

The young man stood in the yard.

"Is there a problem?"

"No, I just wanted to talk to your niece."

He pulled the rake past the young man. He had to stay out of it. How often he'd known that thought. Everything was everyone else's business. He just had to stand aside and listen.

He finished raking the leaves and went into the house to listen for the baby. She was still asleep, but would soon wake. The baby seemed to know when his wife's car turned the corner. She seemed to know when her mother was getting close.

He waited in the kitchen until he heard his wife's car in the garage. She came in the house alone. His niece was at the curb talking to the boy.

He stood at the window, just out of sight. His wife told him not to stare at them, but he didn't leave the window. If the boy tried to make his niece do anything she didn't want to, he'd go out there. In the meantime, he had to watch, unable to hear what they were saying. His wife called him away from the window, but he stayed.

What if he lost them? He and his wife had a life together. He could have his study back. He could get a book when he wanted it, and not have to knock or wait until his niece was gone. He hadn't wanted a baby in the house before his niece's baby. What did it matter? he asked himself.

He thought of stellar gases swirling millions of miles an hour with incredible power to create and destroy stars. The whole universe tumbled in what seemed chaos, but he couldn't bring himself to use that word. The man who heard the land heard his own heart as if it were distant space struggling with its solar dust and clattering, its turbulence on a scale he couldn't comprehend.

He felt his head swirl also.

His niece came in the house crying, and went to her room. The young man's car was gone from the front of the house.

He paced the living room and kitchen. His wife was feeding the baby. Soon she called the niece into the kitchen.

He still paced as he listened to them. The young man had been the baby's father. He hadn't been there when the baby was born. He wouldn't be there for her as she raised the baby. He had told her he knew she could take him to court for child support. But he didn't have anything. He was going to move to Minneapolis, try to find a job. Maybe he could send her something when he had it.

She knew he would not. "He didn't want us," the niece said. "I knew it, but now I've heard him say it." She wiped the tears on her face.

He had known that abandonment. He knew it when he thought of his own mother. Was this the way his father had made his mother feel? Had she cried too? But she had gone off also, like his father, like the young man. Both his parents had.

Was that why he wanted to hold his wife, the niece and baby? They were his family. He hadn't wanted the young man to take them, even though the niece and baby were the young man's family, if he had wanted them. He was glad the young man was gone. He felt like he could have driven the young man away. He would have stood in his way if he tried to take them. His niece would stop crying. Look at the baby his wife was feeding. How it grasped the bottle with its hands. How it stopped to look at his wife and make noises.

Was he standing in their way? Keeping them for himself? Molding their lives to fit his? He thought of the parents who had raised him. He was grateful for their sacrifice, but wasn't he doing what they had done? Nothing was simple, but a mix of complexities. How could he sort out everything?

He stood on the deck and looked at the evening sky while his wife and niece cooked supper and talked. He kept sighing with relief. He saw the V formation of geese above the pines to the south. How could he feel at home in a world that was not his? That had bypassed him?

What was the truth of his life? Did it turn over like the geese flying north or south? He knew there was a point goose, but it was not always on the point. Eventually it fell back and there was another goose to take the lead, and then another, each one falling back and making its way to the front again.

The next time he went to the cemetery to visit his parents' graves, he'd take the baby.

Maybe he would figure out his thoughts someday. He wondered if his father already knew, released from the bonds of this life. What would he know? He would know himself. He would know the land had a voice. He would know whatever else he hadn't understood during his life. Maybe he would even know the universe. He thought of a shifting state of alignment. A flux that operated in imbalance. Maybe that's where he would begin. Maybe those were the words to start or finish his book.

After supper, he made notes in his bedroom. His wife and niece were in the living room talking on the phone to his wife's sister.

The point goose always was there, he wrote. It cut a hole into the air through which the others passed. The point goose was the word. The spoken word. The sound of a voice. Not the object itself, but the sound that cut the air. It was what salvation was about. The holy cutting of the other for others to pass through. The cut saying, *let them pass*. Wasn't that what he heard in church?

He thought of the whole alluvial mess, the mud, the life from water, the suffering at Gethsemane for the pain the world would get itself into. The happening of the world in a word, the spoken into the nothingness, the something of the word that cut the nothing into being, being the spoken word spoken into the narrow point of air.

It was the connection at the same time the separation of it from the other. God spoke the land out of the rubble; his voice was rock. Then rest a moment, spark again the rise of a mysterious mothball up through soda-water gas bubbles into the world. To the edge of the voice getting back on track. The earth turning in space; the density of the universe around it. The unknown fabric in which the world was wrapped; the division of voice into the Babel of tribes on earth; it was what he wrote over which the point goose flew pointing.

Maybe these were thoughts he could use in his "Writings on Faith" course, the one he had taught when the new professor had taken his "Literature and the Environment" course.

There was a brink of the unknown, he continued writing after his wife came into the bedroom. It looked sometimes known, but unraveled the accelerating faster than it had before. The way words couldn't fit together to mean what they should mean. The more that was known the faster it went. He tried again. Where were the missing parts? The unknown force of forces that would make itself known. What was at work? The shifts of light. The unknown quantity. How could it be uncovered? All he needed was a simple unification theory. A box inside a box inside a box inside.

What was this he found? He was reading a new anthology of Native American literature in the Morris university library. There was the story his Indian student had written called, "Raven Steals the Light"!

Before there was anything, before the great flood had covered the earth and receded, before the animals walked the earth or the trees covered the land or the birds flew between the trees, even before the fish and the whales and seals swam in the sea, an old man lived in a house on the bank of a river with his only child, a daughter. What she looked like didn't really matter because the whole world was dark at that time; blacker than a thousand winter nights. She could have been uglier than a sea slug, or lovely as the spring sunrise on hemlock.

The reason the world was dark was the man who lived in the house by the river. He had a box which contained a box which contained a box which contained an infinite number of boxes, each nestled in a box slightly larger than itself, until finally, there was a box so small, it contained all the light in the universe.

The Raven, who existed at that time because he had always existed and always would, was not satisfied with the darkness, since it led to a lot of blundering around and bumping into things.

Eventually, his bumbling in the dark led him to the house of the old man where he heard the man singing. When he fol-

lowed the man's voice, he came to the wall of the house, and there, placing his ear against the planking, he could make out the words, "I have a box and inside the box is another box and inside it are many more boxes, and in the smallest box of all is all the light in the world, and it is all mine and I'll never give it to anyone, not even to my daughter, because, who knows, she may be homely as a slug, and neither she nor I would like to know that."

He looked up as he read the story at the library table. Here was the same story, only developed, or maybe it was the rest of the story, or however it was that a story opened into story and could be told all at once, or in parts, revealing itself in different phases and at different times. When was it the student had written about the light in the boxes? Several years ago? Several quarters ago? Already it was the winter term again. Snow was piled in the corners of the parking lot. It was piled as high as the stack of student papers he always had to grade. If he looked at the snow from the corner of his eye, he thought it was papers falling on him.

He was waiting for his niece to get out of her classes. They could pick up the baby at the church care center and return to the house about the time his wife did.

Was he supposed to stop and pick up anything from the store? No, they had just gone the other night.

He looked at his watch and continued reading:

It took only an instant for the Raven to decide to steal the light for himself, but it took longer for him to invent a way to do it. First he had to find a door into the house. But no matter how many times he circled the wall, the planking remained an unbroken barrier. Sometimes he heard the old man or his daughter leave the house to get water or something else, but they always departed from the side of the house opposite to him, and when he ran around to the other side, the wall seemed unbroken as ever.

As the Raven thought about how he could get into the house, he began to think more and more of the young girl who lived there, and thinking of her began to stir more than just the Raven's imagination.

A student was standing beside the table where he read. She wanted to talk about the paper she was writing. He said he was busy; about ready to leave. Could she come to his office during office hours? He was impatient to get back to the Raven. He dismissed her and she left the table.

He returned to the story:

"It's probable she's homely as a sea slug," the Raven said to himself, "but on the other hand, she may be as beautiful as the fronds of hemlock in the spring sun, if only there were light." And in that idle speculation, he found the solution to his problem.

He waited until the young woman, whose footsteps he could distinguish by now from those of her father, came to the river to gather water. Then he changed himself into a single hemlock needle, dropped himself into the river and floated down just in time to be caught in the basket which the girl was dipping in the river.

Even in his diminished form, the Raven was able to make a small magic, enough to make the girl so thirsty she took a drink from the basket, and in doing so, swallowed the needle.

The Raven slithered down into her warm insides and found a comfortable spot, where he transformed himself once again, this time into a very small human being, and went to sleep for a long time. While he slept he grew.

Another student stood at the table. He wanted to go over his course schedule for the spring quarter. The spring quarter? Hadn't the winter just begun? He told the student to see him in his office and went back to reading:

The young girl didn't have any idea what was happening to her, and of course, she didn't tell her father, who noticed nothing unusual because it was dark, until suddenly he became very aware of a new presence in the house, as the Raven emerged triumphantly in the shape of a human boy.

He was, or would have been, if anyone could have seen him, a strange looking boy, with a long, beaklike nose and a few feathers here and there. In addition, he had the shining eyes of the Raven, which would have given his face a bright, inquisitive appearance, if anyone could have seen him.

And he was noisy. He made all the noises of a spoiled child and an angry raven, yet he could sometimes speak like the wind in the hemlock boughs, with an echo of another sound, a bell, which is part of every raven's speech. At times like this, his grandfather grew to love this strange new member of his household and spent many hours playing with him, making him toys and inventing games for him.

He knew how the grandfather felt as he sat at the table in the university library reading the story. But he wasn't a grandfather to the baby. He was an uncle. A great-uncle.

He looked at his watch, waiting for his niece to come so they could retrieve the baby.

He returned to the story again, hoping no one would bother him:

As the Ravenchild gained more of the affection of the old man, he felt around the house, trying to find where the light was hidden. Finally, he put his hand on the big box which stood in the corner of the house. He cautiously lifted the lid, but could see nothing, and all he could feel was another box. His grandfather heard his precious box being disturbed, and punished the Ravenchild, threatening harsher punishment if he touched the box again.

But the Raven pleaded again and again for the large box. The old man finally gave his grandchild the outermost box. This contented the boy for a short time, but the Raven soon demanded the next box.

It took many tantrums and cajoling, but one by one the boxes were removed. When only a few were left, a strange radiance, never before seen, began to infuse the darkness of the house, disclosing shapes and their shadows, still too dim to have definite form. The Ravenchild then begged in his most pitiful voice to be allowed to hold the light for just a moment.

The Raven's request was instantly refused, but in time, his grandfather yielded. The old man lifted the light, in the form of a beautiful incandescent ball, from the smallest box and tossed it to his grandson.

He only had a glimpse of the child on whom he had lavished his love, for as the light was traveling toward him, the child changed from his human form to a huge, shining black shadow, wings spread and beak open. The Raven snapped up the light in his jaws, thrust his great wings downward and shot through the smokehole of the house into the huge darkness of the world.

Now his niece was at the library table, ready to go. In the middle of the story, he'd have to close the book. No, he could take it with him.

"You ready to go?" he asked.

She nodded.

"I've got to sign out this book. Let's go."

He stopped at the checkout desk while his niece waited. Then she thought of a book she should get.

He continued reading while he waited at the door:

The world was at once transformed. The Raven saw the mountains and valleys. He saw the river sparkle with broken reflections.

Far away, another great winged shape launched itself into the air, as light struck the eyes of the Eagle for the first time and showed him the Raven.

The Raven flew on, rejoicing in his new possession, admiring the effect it had on the world below, reveling in being able to see where he was going, instead of flying blind, only hoping he would get where he was going.

The Raven never saw the Eagle until the Eagle was almost upon him. In a panic he swerved to escape the savage outstretched claws, and in doing so dropped a good half of the light he was carrying. It fell to the rocky ground below and there broke into pieces, one large piece and too many small ones to count. They bounced back into the sky and became the moon and the stars.

But what about the sun? he thought as his niece pulled his arm and they went to the car.

"Where's your book?" he asked.

She wouldn't have time to read tonight, she said. She'd get the book another day.

No, he thought, the sun was the large light still in the Raven's beak. Only the pieces of the half of the light that fell were the moon and stars.

He kept the motor running at the church while the niece went for the baby. Often he went in too, and they would find her sleeping. But now he waited in the car and opened the anthology:

The Eagle pursued the Raven beyond the rim of the world, and there, exhausted by the long chase, the Raven finally let go of his last piece of light, which became the sun.

Its first rays caught the smokehole of the house by the river, where the old man sat weeping bitterly over the loss of his precious light and the treachery of his grandchild. But as the light reached in, he looked up and for the first time saw his daughter, who had been quietly sitting during all this time, completely bewildered by the events.

The old man saw she was beautiful as the fronds of a hemlock against a spring sky at sunrise.

His niece opened the car door and got in with the baby. He looked at them like the old man looked at his daughter.

Was there more to the story? he thought as he drove them home. Would he find a further version in another book somewhere? Would he dream the rest of it, or imagine it somehow? Would it show up when he least expected it? What other meanings could there be? He knew that stories went on and on. They revealed themselves little by little, piece by piece, in different places, at different times. Maybe the good ones had no finish.

Maybe the land was a story so filled with voices it was open to many interpretations. Maybe it went on and on.

He listened to his niece talk to her baby as they turned into the drive and pulled into the garage.

After dinner, he shoveled the front walk. He stood looking up at the stars, which he realized were shining. At the front door, he heard the baby cry as his wife and niece bathed her and got her ready for bed.

He would give her whatever light he had. He would give her the rest of his life. That's what his parents had done: imparted themselves to him, shining all the time, though at times they seemed to him like the darkness between the stars. Maybe that's what he would seem to his niece and her baby, but he would give them the little, dropped pieces of light he found. *They had fallen on the land*, he thought the land said as he went into the house. It was from the land they bounced to the sky.

If only he could see the sky, he thought as he returned to school the next day. It was overcast again. It had been overcast for weeks, except for a few, brief moments. *The clouds covered the land,* he heard the land say. He knew how it felt. It reminded him of when he knew he was not heard. No, he was heard, but not always understood.

He thought of the Indian boarding school established sometime in the 1880s on what was now the Morris campus. The children taken from their families; a new language stuffed in their mouths. It was their sorrow, their anger the land carried. Maybe it was some of the dreariness he felt. It was part of the past he heard when he heard the land. But the school was deeded to the federal government in 1909. And deeded to the state for a university. It was in recognition of the past, and a conscientious commitment to the present—he thought he heard.

The cold front stalled, the weatherman was explaining as he turned into the university parking lot with his niece. But what could he do?

He thought of the land. Underneath were the patterns of conversation. Changing, transmuting, vectoring. Showing several viewpoints—*showing from the other side. More Boys Anything Could Make.* Sometimes he wanted to head upward through the clouds. Retreat. Other times he remained stalled. Sometimes he even moved forward. He was one of those tribes who had possessed Canaan when Israel crossed into the promised land and took it from them. Did the Bible tell the Indian's story? It depended on which way he looked at it. The voice of the land was jointed.

He took his niece's elbow as they crossed an icy patch

of the sidewalk. "We'll eat out tonight," he told her. "How about the Ranch House Restaurant? I'll call my wife to meet us."

"What if the baby fusses?"

"I'll take her to the little waiting room inside the front door."

"I'd rather eat at Ardelle's," she said.

He had his hand on the slippery voice of the land. How indecipherable it was. How wondrous and inconsonant. If only he could understand.

Thanks to Sung Kyu Kim at Macalester College for his "Physics II Contemporary Concepts" course; to *National Geographic*, Vol. 185, No. 1, January 1994, for the article "New Eyes on the Universe" by Bradford A. Smith, and to Connie and Gary Brouillette who let me stay at their house on Lake Lotawana in Missouri where I found the magazine while I was working on the novel; to the *St. Paul Pioneer Press* for news articles about the flood, and especially to Nick Coleman's "Nature's Wrath, Nature's Legacy," April 13, 1997.

Thanks also to P. T. Vance for reading the manuscript and to Jim Turnure for his comments. A special thanks to Nathaniel Hart, professor of English, University of Minnesota at Morris, for his careful reading of the manuscript and his help with details of the university and of Morris.

Acknowledgment is due to *Singing of Earth: A Native American Anthology*, edited by Joseph Bruchac and Diana Landau, Walking Stick Press, the Nature Company, Berkeley, California, 1993, for the Haida story "Raven Steals the Moon;" and to *Native American Literature: An Anthology*, edited by Lawana Trout, NTC Publishing Group, Lincolnwood, Illinois, 1999, for "Raven Steals the Light" by Bill Reid and Robert Bringhurst, originally published by Douglas & McIntyre/University of Washington Press.

The Man Who Heard the Land was designed and set in Akira Kobayashi's typeface Clifford by Will Powers at the Minnesota Historical Society Press. Printed by Maple-Vail Press.